JO-JO

by

ELLA ANDERSON

CHRISTIAN LITERATURE CRUSADE
Fort Washington, Pennsylvania 19034

CHRISTIAN LITERATURE CRUSADE
Fort Washington, Pennsylvania 19034

CANADA
1440 Mackay Street, Montreal, Quebec

First published 1959
Reprinted 1967
This edition 1974 by special arrangement
with the British publisher, Pickering &
Inglis Ltd.

SBN 87508-693-4

CONTENTS

California, Here We Come!

1
"WE'LL BE THERE IN FIFTEEN minutes," Audrey Dean declared excitedly, as she checked her wristwatch. "Think of it! A real Californian ranch with sunshine every day."

"We have sunshine in Canada, too," Esther Chapman, her chum, reminded her with a chuckle, as they sat facing the big windows in the observation car.

"All year round?" Paula Gray giggled from the other side of the car. "I don't think I would like sunshine every day myself, though," she went on doubtfully, gazing out of the window at the heat waves shimmering on the passing orange groves. "Our Canadian winters can be a lot of fun."

The other two heartily agreed, but they had to admit that seeing a Californian ranch was going to be an awful lot of fun, too.

"Sure was nice of Mr. Denton to invite all of us," Paula went on. "He's an old friend of your dad's, isn't he, Audrey?"

Audrey nodded. "For years they lumberjacked in Canada together and then Mr. Denton came down to ranch in San Paloma, where his brother was. Now he is sole owner of the Little Creek Ranch."

"Little Creek Ranch," Esther repeated dreamily. "That name has possibilities."

"For adventure, you mean?"

Esther nodded at Paula. "Why not? Indians or something. . . ."

"In this day and age? Why, gal, you're years out of

date," Audrey chuckled. "Dad says this is a sleepy little place but he thought we would enjoy the horse-back trials. He knows how we love to ride. But as far as adventure is concerned . . ." she shook her head doubtfully.

"Well, I can always hope, you know," Esther returned stoutly.

"If I see any arrow-shooting Indians around, Esther, I'll order up a few for you," Paula promised generously, making them all laugh.

The train's quick clickety-clack was so quietly rhythmic that Audrey began to feel her eyes shutting against her will. Even Paula roused herself with a jerk and chuckled.

"This air is so languid that my eyelids weigh a ton."

"It might help if we went out on the observation platform," Audrey suggested. "Some fresh air would wake us up."

"It's a lovely idea," Esther returned sleepily, "but the thought of using all that energy to stand up and . . ." she didn't finish as her chums started toward her. "Oh, all right if you insist."

"We'd better hurry or we won't have time to see outside," Paula urged, already pushing the glass door to the side and stepping out.

The hot air hit them full in the face, as they followed after Paula, and left them gasping, but after edging toward the railing, they found a slight breeze which helped. Audrey enjoyed watching the rails slide out from underneath the fast-moving train. Esther was peering across the desert, that they were now passing, and shaking her head. Paula, who was leaning against the glass door to keep out of the sun, saw her.

"What's the matter, Esther?"

"Is there anything more lonely-looking than that desert?" she asked mournfully.

The girls followed her pointing finger and saw endless hills of hot white sand that made their eyelids burn and smart.

Audrey nodded. "Dad says it goes on like that for miles . . . the 'small Sahara', they call it."

"The Arabs, who live in the real Sahara, are braver than I thought," Esther replied. "Anybody that can stand that hot white glare for years must be. . . ."

"Think of something cheerful," Audrey interrupted laughing. "Think of Little Creek Ranch and meeting Monica Evans."

"Who is Monica Evans?" Paula asked quickly. "Somebody I should know?"

"Oh, I forgot to tell you, Paula, because you joined us farther along the line, and I had already told Esther."

"Go on," Paula urged. "Is she a teacher?"

"Oh, no, just a kid like ourselves," Audrey explained. "Her Dad is manager of Little Creek Ranch and takes care of the horses for Mr. Denton, who is much older. Monica is a trick rider like you see in rodeos."

"Trick rider?" Paula echoed. "She must be good. It takes lots of training and nerve, besides having a good horse."

Esther took it up. "I wonder what kind of horses they have?"

Audrey glanced at her watch again. "We'll soon find out in about another five minutes."

"Look! Real cowboys, girls!" Esther shouted suddenly and the other two peered into the distance where she was pointing excitedly.

At first it looked just like a dust cloud, but the thundering sound that became louder showed up finally as ten riders. They were obviously cowboys with their checked shirts and sombreros. They were travelling fast and furious along the side of the tracks, and the dust they kicked up seemed to stay up in the air for a few minutes before finally settling back down again.

"I think they're going to pass us," Paula mumbled. "The train is slowing up now so they could do it quite easily."

"I wonder where they're going?"

Nobody could think of an answer to Audrey's question.

"I'm more curious to know where they came from?" Esther put in. "It's miles since we've seen a ranch."

By now the riders were almost level with them and they could see that the men were hot, tired and that their faces were heavily streaked with grime. They paid no attention to the train but went thundering past it.

"They've been working hard by the looks of them," Audrey put in. "Imagine having to work under this broiling sun, though. . . ."

The other two crowded again to the edge of the railing, but the heat waves danced up and down in front of their eyes making them water. Again they could hear the thundering sound.

"I can't see anything," Audrey grumbled, frowning intensely at the dust cloud. "How can you . . ." she stopped as the three riders, that Paula had glimpsed, materialised out of the dust cloud. "Oh, I see them now."

"They're not Americans anyway," Esther put in confidently. "They seem darker in colouring."

"Mexicans," Audrey explained. "Look at their

8

clothes!" she whispered, as they galloped nearer. "Their sombreros are the pointed kind of the Mexicans, and so are their spurs."

Before the men had quite reached the train, the glass door was pushed open and Mr. Dean stepped out. A tall, heavily-built man with slightly greying hair and a sunburned face that spoke of his outdoor life in Canada.

"Aren't you going to get off at San Paloma with us?" he grinned. "Or are you planning to ride straight down to the Mexican Border?"

Audrey drew her eyes away from the advancing horsemen and stared at her dad. "We are close to the border, aren't we?"

"Just a stone's throw practically," he assured her.

"Can you go over into Mexico any time you want to?" Audrey wanted to know.

Her dad turned and looked at her. "Of course you can," he replied.

"But I thought there was a Border Patrol . . . or something like that."

Mr. Dean nodded. "That's true, but your baggage is searched when you get to the border and then, if you aren't trying to smuggle anything into Mexico," he said with a grin, "you are allowed through."

"What about Mexican cowboys who work on the United States side?" Esther asked.

"They are in a different position," he replied. "As Mexicans, they can go back and forth to work."

"I suppose they are hired a lot on ranches over here," Audrey remarked, keeping an eye on the nearby riders.

"Well, I imagine they are," her dad agreed. "The population is small so far south, and then lots of them work in Hollywood, too."

"We saw some American cowboys pass the train a few minutes ago," Paula put in. "They looked so hot and tired."

"It's a hard life," Mr. Dean told them. "Their dream of owning a ranch some day doesn't always materialise . . . but it's a life they understand and love."

"These cowboys are Mexicans, aren't they, Mr. Dean?" Paula asked, indicating the riders.

Mr. Dean peered intently at them and nodded. "Yes. Probably going home again."

"Well, I suppose we better get ourselves together," Audrey replied practically, and the other two turned with her. Mr. Dean had already gone back through the glass door and Esther and Paula followed. Audrey, who had turned once more to look at the riders, saw they were now alongside the train.

She didn't get much of a glimpse of the first two rider's faces, but the third brought a gasp as the evil leer from the dark eyes, nearly hidden under a huge sombrero, made her shudder with fear.

Hurrying through after the others, she felt a strange feeling of danger steal over her that she couldn't seem to shake off. Perhaps it was just as well that she didn't know what lay ahead for all of them, or her first glimpse of sleepy little San Paloma might have been spoiled.

Little Creek Ranch

2

THE SMALL STATION AT SAN PALOMA was crowded as Audrey and the others gathered together outside on the platform, but a closer look showed that most of them were sightseers who had come in to watch the advent of the arrivals. The air was warm and heavy, and the sweet smell of oranges and lemons seemed to pervade the whole building. Trunks, suitcases and crates were being unloaded from the train, and shy youngsters crowded nearer for a better look at everything. The girls noted the amount of Indians there were, too. Paula caught Esther's eyes and chuckled.

"These Indians too tame for you?"

Esther tossed her head and laughed. "You never know . . . adventure might be just around the corner."

Audrey alone did not smile. A sudden flash-back to the Mexicans gave her again that queer sensation of fright. She shook if off. Imagination running riot, she accused herself mentally. Probably all Mexicans looked like that. She turned as her father gave a sudden shout and saw him signalling another man farther along, who was peering curiously into all the train windows as if looking for someone.

"Is that Mr. Denton?" she whispered.

"The man himself," her dad returned promptly, hurrying toward the other with outstretched hand.

The girls watched as the two men stood pumping hands up and down, and smiled at their enthusiastic greeting. A little farther over, a slightly-built girl wearing riding clothes was standing watching the two men with a smile on her thin, brown face. Suddenly Mr. Dean remembered the others and turned round to wave them on. Mr. Chapman was already shaking hands with the owner of the ranch as the girls sidled shyly up. They surveyed the strange girl with a smile.

"This is Monica," Mr. Dean introduced quickly and Audrey stepped forward.

"Hello, Monica," she greeted.

The other girl, after a slight hesitation, came forward and murmured "Hi!" to one and all of the girls. Mr. Denton proved to be an older edition of Mr. Dean himself, his white hair circling his head like a halo and his bronze skin telling of the many hours he spent outdoors.

"Monica and I thought we had missed you, or that you had taken another train," Mr. Denton remarked as he steered Mr. Dean and Mr. Chapman by the elbow through the crowd that was still watching the train. "Don't bother with the luggage. Out truck will pick it up later," he added as Mr. Chapman hesitated.

As the three men marched ahead, Monica was left alone with the three girls. She was shy and uneasy and Audrey quickly took her by the arm and followed the men, with Paula and Esther following quickly behind them.

"We had the most wonderful trip down," Audrey chatted brightly, trying desperately to put the other girl at her ease. She could see she wasn't used to having many people of her own age around her.

"We stopped off at the place where they keep the famous Palomino ranch horses," Paula called out. "They're marvellous, aren't they?"

They had now left the semi-coolness of the station and found themselves in the fierce glare of the hot sun. Monica turned and Audrey saw an eager light spring up in the girl's brown eyes at the mere mention of horses.

"They're famous in California, although they really come from Texas," she drawled and the girls smiled at her accent. "I have a wonderful horse, too." she went on and then stopped. "I mean, Mr. Denton has, but Dad and I have trained him to do all kinds of tricks . . . he's as smart as a whip," she added proudly. "He's a Palomino, too."

"What's his name?" Esther queried, as they stopped to let some trucks of luggage get by.

"Jo-Jo!" was the prompt reply.

"I like that," Audrey approved, as they started walking again. "We're hoping to do some riding ourselves . . . if we can, of course," she added hastily, but Monica was nodding.

"Mr. Denton and Dad have three fine bays ready for you."

"We heard you were a trick rider, Monica," Audrey remarked. "I hope we get to see you perform."

Monica nodded eagerly. "Jo-Jo and I do a lot of practising and you can be our audience."

Audrey saw that the more this girl talked about Jo-Jo the less embarrassed she was. This Palomino meant everything to her, that was evident.

They were walking toward the end of the sidewalk now and the girls were impressed by the white sandy look of everything. The hot glare of the sun emphasised the adobe walls of the dwellings around them, and the brightly-coloured roofs seemed to burn brilliantly against the pure white walls that supported them. It made the eyes sting to look at them too long.

"The sun makes everything hazy, doesn't it?" Esther remarked suddenly, as they joined the men, now standing before a large touring car.

"You'll probably feel the heat a lot," Monica murmured half-apologetic. "But you get used to it."

"We have some pretty hot summers in Canada, too," Audrey returned with a smile. "But they don't last all year round like they do down here."

The girls scrambled into the back seat of the touring car and pulled down some little extra seats, that were attached at the back end of the front seats, for Paula and Esther, who were giggling with anticipation. The men squeezed into the front seats and Mr. Denton, making sure that the girls were all safely tucked in, started up the engine.

The station was situated a little way out of the town and, as the car descended the hill into San Paloma, Audrey was reminded of the stories of the old Wild West she used to try and read. A few shops with fine city-fashioned clothes were on display and these seemed strangely out of place, being next to a saddler's shop, blacksmith and a small narrow two-storey building with SHERIFF'S OFFICE painted on the glass door. People walking slowly and quietly along the narrow sidewalks were mostly dressed in ranch clothes. But it was the sleepy air of the place that amused Audrey.

"San Diego isn't far away," Monica explained, when Audrey mentioned it. "But to look at this place, you would think it was in another state."

"I like it that way," Esther put in stoutly.

The car drove slowly through the one main street,

creating quite a dust with its wheels. People stood waiting till they passed, and the girls saw them smile at Monica and glance curiously at them.

Soon they were out of San Paloma and driving along the beautiful wide highway on their way to the ranch. The sweet smell of orange blossoms drifted gently in the open windows from the fruit groves on each side, making the girls gulp in deep breaths of it. The ride was short though, much to Audrey's disappointment, who liked the feeling of skimming through this scented air.

"We're nearly there now," Monica announced, as Mr. Denton suddenly turned the car into a small roadway. She pointed in the distance. "You can see Little Creek Ranch from the top of this hill." The girls bent forward and peered. They could just see it as they finally reached the top of the hill. It was a spacious stone built ranch house surrounded by orchards and very beautiful trees. On one side was the well-built bunkhouse, timber cabins, poled corrals and stock pens. It looked a massive place. The girls glanced at each other in surprise. It was much more grand than they had expected.

Mr. Denton was talking animatedly about his prize cattle and horses, with Monica nodding in agreement to the girls. When Jo-Jo was mentioned, Monica clasped her small, capable, tanned hands together in keen pleasure. Andrey noticed the gesture and understood that ranch life was all this girl really cared for, and that she definitely looked capable enough to be able to stand such a hard life.

As they whirled in on a cloud of dust, a stout, motherly woman appeared in the doorway with her hands folded over her apron. Audrey liked Mrs.

Denton immediately and saw that her chums agreed. Monica flew up to her and whirled her around, introducing the girls breathlessly.

Mrs. Denton laughed. "Now you'll have fun showing the girls your trick horse, Jo-Jo," she commented.

And it wasn't long before Monica found an excuse for taking the girls across the yard and up to the enclosure where a proud Palomino stood at the far side. Monica gave a slight whistle and it trotted over quickly to her. It was a light blonde chestnut colour with a very light, almost white, mane and tail and prominent white markings. It tossed its head regally and the girls exclaimed in delight when its thick mane and tail billowed out.

"These horses are all parade and show horses," Monica explained eagerly, as she stroked its nose affectionately. "It is sometimes called 'the peacock of the horse world'."

"It resembles an Arabian or Thoroughbred," Audrey commented, as they walked around it.

"It loves our admiration, doesn't it?" Paula laughed, as it lowered its head for their caresses.

"There's a big Rodeo on tomorrow," Monica went on eagerly. "If you girls would like it, I'll try and get you a place in the Big Parade with me."

"The Big Parade?" Esther echoed wonderingly.

"Every girl rider who can ride at all wants to ride in that parade," Monica explained. "But I'm not going to tell you what it's like . . . I want it to be a surprise." The animated expression on the California girl's face showed how little fun she had had in the past with sharing her joys, and Audrey made a mental note to keep her like this all through their visit.

Later, when the girls were taken upstairs and shown their huge room that held two wide double beds, Monica sank into one of the armchairs and sighed contentedly.

"It sure is going to be a lot of fun having you all here."

"We're so grateful to Mr. Denton for asking us, Monica," Audrey replied. "We want you to show us everything. . . ."

"And throw in at least one adventure for Esther," Paula broke in quickly.

Monica looked at her and Esther wonderingly. Esther explained the reason for the remark, but Monica shook her head.

"I'm afraid nothing ever happens here," she said. "It used to be wild with bandits years ago but I'm afraid that's all over." Esther looked disappointed. "But we'll find some excitement for you, though," she added with a grin.

As Monica helped the girls to unpack, a small book jumped out of her hand that she had picked up out of a suitcase. She glanced at it curiously and then stared incredulously when she saw it was a small, neat Bible. She laid it down hastily and turned to do something else, but not before Audrey had seen her. But when the other girls put their own books beside their bed, Monica frowned thoughtfully.

"You girls are Christians, aren't you?" she asked at last. They nodded eagerly in reply.

"Are you, Monica?" Audrey asked bluntly.

Monica shook her head. "I don't know. I've never thought much about it. I believe in God, of course, but I can't see that it matters much just as long as you do your best."

"But you never get to know your Heavenly Father well if you just take Him for granted," Audrey retorted, stung by such a lack of interest.

Monica looked at her in surprise. "I'm sorry, Audrey," she apologised with a shrug. "But I'm afraid that's the way I feel."

The girls dropped the subject then, but Audrey promised herself that she would make Monica see it their way before she left Little Creek Ranch.

Pedro Lorenzo

3

WHEN THE GIRLS AWOKE THE NEXT morning they found the sun streaming in, bright and hot, through their large window. The lowing of cattle, the shouts of men working, and the faint barking of a dog came drifting gently in, reminding them where they were.

Audrey lay trying to remember what had been planned for the day's program. Suddenly it dawned on her and she excitedly called to the others. The Rodeo! They had rodeos in Canada, too, but they were a little different, she had been told.

"I'm so eager to see Monica do her trick riding and . . ." Audrey broke off and looked around the room. "By the way, where is she?"

Esther, who had been paired off with Monica, shook her head. "She must have gone out early to practice."

"She's nice, isn't she?" Audrey murmured, as with her hands behind her head she lay back and looked up at the ceiling. "She was awfully shy at first, but I think she has got over it now."

Esther nodded over. "Just mention Jo-Jo and she forgets her shyness immediately. He is a beautiful horse and I don't blame her for being so enthusiastic about him."

"Pancakes and syrup," Paula murmured dreamily and Audrey looked down at her sharply. Paula caught her look and grinned. "Sniff deeply and tell me I'm wrong," she challenged.

Audrey did as she was told and sighed contentedly. "Just the thing to start the day off with," she agreed.

"I can't stand it any longer," Paula remarked, slipping out of bed and over to the window. Suddenly she waved to the others. "Look! There's Monica now!"

In a flash the girls were crowding around the window and peering down on to the yard below, where they could see Jo-Jo racing round in dizzy circles with Monica hanging perilously on to his back. As the horse flashed toward the house, Monica looked up and saw the three eager faces watching her. With a wave of her hand, she shot off Jo-Jo's back on to the edge of the fence and bowed to them. They clapped wildly down to her, although Audrey's eyes had nearly popped out and Esther had given a little scream of fright. Paula chuckled nervously.

"If she performs like that this afternoon, we're going to have some excitement." She paused. "I wonder if she got us a place beside her . . . and if she did, what are we going to wear?"

"One worry at a time, please," Audrey ordered with a laugh. "I'm quite sure Monica doesn't expect us to ride in our white linen suits, or even our own ordinary riding clothes."

And she was right. No sooner had the girls tripped down, when the breakfast gong sounded, than Monica was sitting beside them telling about her plans for them. Audrey watched her thin, expressive face and wondered thoughfully how she was going to make this girl see their way of working for their Saviour. They were all true witnesses for their Lord Jesus Christ.

"Aren't you eager to come, Audrey?" Monica's voice snapped Audrey's mind back to the table again.

She smiled. "I can hardly wait, Monica. What we saw from our window convinced us that we don't want to miss a thing. You and Jo-Jo will steal the show."

Monica, whose expression had looked worried at Audrey's inattention, brightened up again at Audrey's words.

"I have the nicest cowgirl outfits for you all to wear, too . . . just wait till you see them."

"I told the girls you would have something planned for us," Audrey replied, and Monica looked happy at the sincere compliment.

Quietness reigned for a little while as Mrs. Denton came in with a huge platter of steaming pancakes and warned them not to waste too much time talking, for they were to leave right away.

"Aren't you coming, too, Mrs. Denton?" Audrey asked shyly, but the older woman smiled and shook her head.

"No. I've seen so many rodeos in my day, Audrey, that I can afford to stay home," she laughed. "The dust and hot sun are just too much for me now."

"We'll bring you back a lovely present," Paula promised.

"I'll try to bring back the silver cup for you," Monica chuckled.

"You just do that, honey," Mrs. Denton laughed and handed Audrey the jug of syrup.

As Monica laid the outfits on the two beds right after breakfast, the girls were more than excited at the thought of wearing them. There was a regular scramble as each girl picked out the one best suited to her, and Audrey chuckled as she put on her Stetson before the mirror.

"I'm an old cowhand," she warbled in Western fashion, and the others capered around her, with Monica sitting on the floor and clapping her hands joyously as each one got into her outfit and found it a perfect fit.

"I'm so thankful that we are all about the same height," Monica breathed. "Dad telephoned the Rodeo Grounds early this morning and made arrangements for all of us to be together in the Big Parade."

Monica bowed to herself in the mirror as, dressed in green skirt, orange satin blouse with fringed chaps and her white Stetson, she waited for the others.

"My, I don't believe it," she murmured, her blue eyes sparkling with anticipation. The orange blouse had taken her breath away at first, but it did show off that blue-black, slightly wavy hair of hers. She chuckled at Esther, standing beside her.

Esther grinned back as, in a navy-blue skirt and emerald satin blouse, she waved her Stetson in the air. The emerald satin showed the short mahogany-coloured curls to advantage. Even Paula, who couldn't stop giggling, looked grand in her dark brown skirt and bright pink satin blouse, her light brown hair looking coppery coloured in contrast. Monica grinned when she caught their admiring eyes as she pulled on her gloves. Her black skirt and pure white satin blouse, with glittering rhinestones patterned all over it, brought gasps of admiration from her onlookers.

"I'm goin' to sparkle, gals," she drawled, as a ray of the sun turned her whole blouse into one sparkling jewel. "All performers wear rhinestones somewhere on their outfits so that they sparkle and glitter when they do their acts. The crowd expects it."

"You'll sparkle without rhinestones," Esther declared stoutly as she slapped on her own Stetson and picked up her fringed white gloves, like all the rest had on. "Let's get goin' to that there Rodeo," she drawled, and Monica howled at her imitation of a western cowboy.

But the three girls gasped in amazement when they went downstairs and out into the yard, for there stood Jo-Jo in all his splendour, the small rhinestones on his brand new saddle glittering brightly as the sun hit them. He seemed to know how fancy he looked for he pranced on his dainty feet and tossed his lovely head with pride.

At last, Mr. Evans, a small, stout man with a continuous grin on his face, came and led Jo-Jo away to his box car on a truck, and Monica hurried the girls over to four beautiful bays that were waiting patiently to be noticed.

"I'm riding one, too," Monica explained. "We mustn't tire Jo-Jo for he has a big programme ahead of him."

Riding slowly behind the truck, a few minutes later, gave the girls a feeling of already being in the Rodeo. Only when Audrey turned around in her saddle and saw her Dad and Mr. Chapman with Mr. Denton driving the big car that was following, did it remind her that they hadn't reached the Grounds yet.

The air was cool and sweet and the sun was just warm enough to be comfortable. The distant mountains still had a grey misty look, which only brought out the objects nearer to them with a clearer outline. Audrey took a deep breath of the mountain air and thought they were all just about the four happiest girls that could be found. Some of her placid content was mirrored on the other girl's faces, too. Even Monica, who had been nervously dashing around to make sure everything was brought along that would be needed, was now gazing around her with a calm peaceful look that would certainly help her nerves with that dangerous performance that was yet to come.

They rode into San Paloma and found the quiet little village astir and bustling with preparations for the Rodeo, that was being held not too far away. Mr. Evans had to slow the truck down to let people cross over, and they waved and called out to him. Monica waved her Stetson and got three rousing cheers from some very small girl admirers on the sidewalk, who were dreaming of the day when they, too, would be dressed up as she was and going to perform on their own pet horses.

But their arrival at the Rodeo Grounds really mounted their excitement. There were people everywhere, crowding along the narrow street and stepping nimbly up on the board sidewalks to prevent themselves from being knocked over by cars and horses. The girls didn't get much time to take in all the noise and bustle before the truck ahead suddenly swerved to the left while Monica, in the lead now, went straight on.

A good-sized hotel was straight ahead and to this she led them with the big car in their wake. Audrey cast excited glances at Esther and Paula and saw them grinning happily at those on the sidewalks, who were returning their smiles and waving to them.

Even the hotel itself was packed with all kinds of people, dressed in various styles of clothes from Western to purely New England.

24

"I'm so excited," Audrey murmured to Monica, as they all stood waiting for Mr. Denton to sign the register.

"Wait till tomorrow," Monica whispered back. "I'm enjoying all this through you and the other girls' eyes. Don't forget, this is all old hat to me."

"But you're enjoying it just the same," Esther laughed. "Your eyes are glittering like your blouse."

Monica laughed. When Mr. Denton joined them again, and they were all finally settled in their rooms, Monica suggested taking a quick walk before lunch.

"We have nearly an hour, and it might be too hot in the afternoon for much walking about."

The girls thought this a great idea and in a few minutes they were hurrying back down the hotel steps and along the board sidewalk. They had to walk double and Audrey laughed to Monica when she was pushed off about a dozen times, while Esther giggled as she ran to rescue her Stetson that was in danger of being tossed into the street. On one side of the street were gaily decorated shops, bright with colour, cheery as to sound and happy with the spirit of anticipation. On the other side were the Grounds that they would see better tomorrow, when all the activities would be centred there.

Men and women, singly, in pairs, and in groups, thronged the walk beside them. Six-gallon hats, shiny and studded leather belts, satin shirts as bright as the girls' own, and the constant click of high-heeled boots of the cowboys on the wooden street, rang merrily in their ears.

The Canadian girls had been shy at first to appear

in such bright colours, but as Audrey laughed and remarked later, "We were dull compared to some of those checked shirts the cowboys were wearing."

They were just approaching a small cafe when a group of dark-skinned cowboys came hurrying out of it and charged right in front of them. All of the girls stopped quickly and looked at them. Audrey frowned at their rudeness. They might, at least, have apologised for not looking where they were going, she thought angrily, when suddenly one of them turned and glanced back at the girls. Audrey's heart shot to her throat in terror. She gasped and Monica, who was walking beside her, glanced at her curiously.

"That Mexican cowboy," Audrey whispered, indicating the backs of the men as they hurried across the street. "The last one . . . I saw him riding along beside our train, and I don't know why but he gives me the shivers."

Monica smiled and glanced casually at the cowboys. "They're all Mexicans and . . ." she stopped abruptly and Audrey saw her stare incredulously at them. Turning her head quickly, Audrey was just in time to see the three cowboys, who were now standing on the other side of the street, turn abruptly away and disappear in the crowd.

"What is it, Monica?" Esther whispered. "You look white."

"That last cowboy you pointed out," Monica gasped out. "I'm positive he's the professional horsethief who was ordered out of this country last year. His name is Pedro Lorenzo." She walked silently along for a few minutes then suddenly she spoke again. "If he's back here again it can only mean one thing." She paused and the girls stopped walking and listened intently.   "He has his eye on some fine horse in the Rodeo tomorrow."

Monica's Warning

4   AUDREY FELT A COLD FEELING OF dread hit her at Monica's last remark. Somehow, she had a strange premonition about this Rodeo tomorrow. Even when she tried to switch her mind on to some brighter thought, Monica's quiet set face beside her spoiled the effort.

"Are you worrying about Jo-Jo?" she asked quietly, and Monica nodded without speaking. "But aren't there other Palomino horses that are trained like Jo-Jo?"

Monica shook her head. "No. Palominos are show or parade horses, as I mentioned before, but not many owners bother to train them for anything special. Jo-Jo has been well trained and could bring in a mint of money if he was put up for auction."

"Any other horses of value here that you know of?" Esther asked, as she and Paula slowed up in front to catch what Monica was saying.

"There may be, Esther," Monica replied uncertainly. "I don't know of any in particular, but I think I'd better warn Dad anyway."

The girls looked over apprehensively at the Grounds across the street. Would Mr. Evans be able to take care of Jo-Jo well enough? Even if he was expecting trouble, would he be able to handle the situation? He couldn't be with Jo-Jo all the time.

They crossed the street without saying anything, being careful not to get in the way of several horses that were now prancing past them. Audrey had to smile in spite of herself, as the horses, gay with ribbons and noisy as to bells, bobbed their heads and turned in at the big gate where Jo-Jo's truck had gone previously.

It was all so exciting and looked like there would be lots of fun, that it did seem particularly awful to be worrying about someone stealing Jo-Jo. The irritating thought flashed through Audrey's mind as Monica took the lead once more when they had reached the sidewalk in safety.

"I hope Dad hasn't left yet," Monica murmured and slipped in the gate with the others close behind her. The dust was so thick in the air from the horse's hoofs that Audrey could feel it gritting on her teeth. Screwing up their eyes they kept Monica's quick-moving figure in sight.

Horse trucks, cattle trucks, trucks full of equipment were either parked or moving in a slow line while their drivers peered through the dust to find places to stop. Monica seemed to know where she was going, for she plodded doggedly ahead turning round once in a while to make sure the others were following.

"He generally parks on the other side," she gasped, and Audrey nodded without speaking.

The dust was curling up all around them now with choking intensity as four young Shetland ponies tore past with such an unexpected burst of speed that the girls had to laugh in spite of themselves.

"I hope it isn't like this on the Parade Ground," Paula gurgled. "I won't be able to see a thing."

"It's always this way on this side, Paula," Monica comforted. "The ground on the other side of the Arena is harder and you don't have trucks tearing it up either."

"That's a comfort," Esther choked behind her handkerchief.

"There's Dad!" Monica shouted suddenly and quickly hurried away with the others blindly following. "He sees us," she called back over her shoulder and Audrey nodded.

"I don't see how he can in this dust storm," Esther grumbled.

Mr. Evans' face held a curious look as he watched their approach. He looked at his daughter.

"It's dangerous to come here, Monica," he said disapprovingly. "You could easily get hurt."

"I know that, Dad," Monica replied. "We just had to come to tell you something, though."

"Tell me what?"

Monica had to swallow to find her voice, for the dust had choked her up completely. At last she managed it and began to explain. As soon as she mentioned Pedro Lorenzo's name Mr. Evans' face changed from his smiling, listening attitude to one of shocked disbelief. He shook his head when she had finished.

"I think you must have been mistaken, Monica," he replied dubiously. "Pedro was sent out of this country last year and you know the Sheriff waits till they are completely over the Border and then a watch is kept for a long time afterwards."

"Couldn't he get back in again after the Sheriff had left?" Audrey asked puzzled.

"Pretty hard to cross the Border when you have already been ordered out, for the Patrols have been warned to watch out for you again," Mr. Evans returned quickly. "Even if he did get in, how is he going to smuggle a horse like Jo-Jo out again? He's noticeable miles away. His colour alone would give him away . . . he's so pale."

They all stood silently looking at Mr. Evans now,

who was frowning at the ground in deep thought. Suddenly he looked up and smiled as he caught their serious faces.

"Well, just go back to the hotel and don't worry about it," he told them. "You've told me about it and I'll keep an eye on him . . . just in case it is Jo-Jo that Pedro is after. We won't even bother Mr. Denton about it until we're sure."

They smiled in relief at his confident voice and hurried out again. Monica was wearing her bright smile again.

"Now that I know Dad knows all about it . . . I feel lots better," she confided. "He'll have two other men to help him anyway, so Jo-Jo shouldn't be alone for a minute."

Back on the board walk again, they began to feel better. They had done something definite about protecting Jo-Jo. Audrey was secretly glad that Mr. Evans had believed them for horse thieving in this day and age seemed so remote, and yet it might be that that was the very reason that this Pedro Lorenzo might get away with it.

"Don't look so serious," Monica whispered to her. "Jo-Jo might not even be in any danger anyway."

"I was thinking that horse thieves seem so out-of-date somehow," Audrey confessed. "So unreal, if you know what I mean."

"They're real enough down here," Monica returned drily. "A good horse is a good horse in any century. They get wonderful prices in Mexico, too, where no questions are asked about ownership."

Audrey nodded and remained silent. It was like something in a Western story. And it fitted in with everyone dressed up in the old-time Western style for the occasion. Groups of young people arm-in-arm were spread out on the sidewalk and closed in as they neared them, their bright sunburned and tanned faces sparkling with the anticipation of what was coming Their happy attitude brightened up the four who were walking along so serious-looking. Some roasting peanuts from a nearby shop reminded them that they were hungry and, resisting the temptation to go in and buy some, they turned and fairly flew back to the hotel for lunch.

As Monica had warned, the afternoon was too warm for much walking about. Waiting until it was lots cooler, in the evening, the girls came out of the hotel and strolled once more on the wooden sidewalk. There seemed to be more people than ever and from a little distance they could see a deep red glow turn the night sky into a rosy pink colour.

Curious, they hurried along to it and found that a huge bonfire had just been lit and was now really at its brightest. The heat from it kept the crowds at a fairly safe distance. Suddenly a loud hissing and crackling sound farther over drove the four girls to investigate. They found that groups of cowboys and cowgirls were sending up rockets and flares. The sky was dazzling with firecracker lights and Audrey kept blinking whenever a particularly bright one went off near her.

Sparklers were handed to them by a nearby cowboy and, feeling like a lot of kids on a holiday, they waved them about. They had plenty of company, too, in the crowd for the cowboy had generously supplied others.

At last, weary and exhausted, Monica took them into the little shop that had smelled so appetisingly of roasting peanuts earlier that day, and ordered all kinds of ice cream sundaes until Audrey warned her that she would be riding alone in the Big Parade.

Audrey was surprised to find how tired she was as, later, the girls gathered in their huge room and prepared for sleep.

"I feel as if I had been riding all day instead of just walking up and down that board walk outside and. . . ."

"And eating everything we saw that looked good," Esther supplied as Audrey paused, and they all heartily agreed.

The next morning found the four girls up bright and early and getting into their gay outfits again. The sun was shining through their hotel window and the air of anticipation was at its highest. They didn't talk much at first as each girl dashed around trying not to keep the others waiting.

"I'm so keyed up you would think it was me that was riding Jo-Jo," Esther giggled, as she kept dropping everything she picked up. "Some riding star I would make."

"I know just how you feel, Esther," Paula took it up. "I'm shivering with excitement and look at the temperature . . . nearly eighty."

Audrey was watching Monica thoughtfully as she stood aside, waiting for the others. Last night she had meant to take up the subject of being a Christian again, but somehow it hadn't seemed the right time. Monica was jumpy about her performance that was coming up, and Audrey han't forgotten her careless shrug when she had mentioned about being a Christian.

Monica had lain with her eyes shut as the girls sat for a few minutes reading their verse out of their Bibles, just like they always did. It had taken a lot of control for Audrey not to ask Monica to join them. But her sleeping attitude had answered her question. *Monica wasn't interested!*

It was just as they were leaving that Audrey decided to try again.

"I hope you win that silver cup, Monica," she said as Monica adjusted her Stetson in front of the mirror. "You said you had tried before in this contest, didn't you?"

Monica turned from the mirror and nodded. "Tried for three years . . . but I won't give up," she added with a chuckle. "I'm improving every year."

"I prayed you would . . . because it means so much to you," Audrey returned very quietly. Esther and Paula stood still, listening intently. Monica flushed as she looked into Audrey's serious eyes.

"Thanks!" she murmured uncomfortably. "That should help."

"Why does it mean so much to you?" Paula asked quickly as the silence lengthened.

Monica turned to her. "It means that if I do get the cup I'll be asked to do performances and perhaps to earn enough to buy Jo-Jo . . . he's still Mr. Denton's horse, you know," she added with a laugh.

"He's a fine horse," Esther murmured.

Monica nodded. "I could earn enough with him to let my Dad retire. He's getting too old for handling horses."

Audrey smiled over to her. "With that unselfish thought in mind, you'll make it," she told her and turned toward the door. Monica followed with a puzzled look on her face, while Esther and Paula exchanged glances.

Nothing more was said until the girls were in the

34

lobby. Audrey had noticed Monica's quick little glances at her, as if she wanted to say something but didn't quite know how to say it. Audrey walked beside her, waiting.

Finally Monica spoke. "You kids really believe there is more to just doing your best, don't you?"

"Of course," Audrey replied quickly. "It's a lonely way to live, I think." She shrugged. "We do our best, too, but we have the fun and joy of knowing that our Heavenly Father is rejoicing with us and that we can ask Him or thank Him for things, while you just go drearily on 'doing your best' and letting it go at that."

Audrey caught a glimpse of Esther and Paula. They were deliberately keeping away so she could talk to Monica.

"I see what you mean all right," Monica's voice brought Audrey's attention back to her. "But you kids have such a wonderful faith that He will help you. I don't believe I could have such deep faith, even if anything really serious was to happen to me."

"You'd be surprised," Audrey returned, and did not know how soon she was to prove that remark.

The Rodeo

5

OUTSIDE THE HOTEL, THEY MET MR.
Dean, Mr. Chapman and Mr. Denton. Audrey's dad
grinned at them.

"Have yourselves a good breakfast?" he inquired.
"Or did you all eat too much last night," he added
mischievously.

"We managed to squeeze in a breakfast," Audrey
chuckled, as they turned toward the Parade Grounds.

If the girls had thought the town packed the day
before, it was nothing to what it was now. The bright
morning sun was making everything dazzle before their
eyes as they walked quickly along. Loud voices
shouting to one another, car horns honking to warn
careless pedestrians that the middle of the road was
the wrong place to walk, young people singing cowboy
songs. Even radios from small shops were blaring
forth their various assortments of programs, while
children played the most energetic of games practically
under the feet of the passing throng.

The air of excitement was catching and the girls,
although serious at first, were soon eagerly looking at
everything. The Grounds were packed and looked
quite different from the day before, when all they
could see was dust. Audrey's dad, with Mr. Chapman,
followed Mr. Denton over to one of the grandstand
seats bidding the girls goodbye, while Monica, her
thin tanned face glowing with excitement, hurried the
girls toward the far end of the Grounds.

"They'll be waiting for us, so we better not be late," she warned.

Audrey felt slightly self-conscious as she and the others walked quickly along in front of the grandstand to where there seemed to be some kind of dug-out. People were shouting and calling down to them as they passed, and Audrey felt her face flush with embarrassment. Esther's giggle and Paula's gasps were audible to Audrey as she kept Monica's fastly disappearing figure in sight.

"There's Jo-Jo!" Monica declared proudly and started to run.

"Don't let her get out of sight," Esther giggled, as she started after her.

Breathless they all arrived at the dug-out and found the line-up of horses all ready to start the Grand March.

"Hurry!" Monica breathed and dashed past the crowd of stamping horses that held every kind of rider imaginable. "They're ready to start!"

In a flash, the three girls dashed after her and then suddenly stopped when a tall girl came forward and grinned to them.

"Here's your horses," she drawled, and Audrey turned to find three beautiful black Arab steeds.

"Lovely!" Audrey breathed, and the girl nodded.

"All the horses in the Parade are culled from the best in the country," she told her proudly and gave her a hand up.

Audrey turned to find Monica beside her, sitting on Jo-Jo, who looked ready for anything as he pranced about nervously. Behind them sat Esther and Paula, who were quietly watching everything.

"Audrey!" Monica called over. "I want you to meet

the Queen of the Rodeo . . . Jess Martin! This is Audrey Dean I was telling you about," she added, and Audrey turned and found a beautiful white horse with a girl rider sitting on it, also in white. The girl smiled brightly and leaned over to shake hands with her. "Hi! I hear you're from Canada, Audrey," Audrey nodded. "So am I . . . Montreal way."

"We're from British Columbia," Audrey murmured, still gazing admiringly at the girl in her beautiful white doeskin breeches and white jacket. The sombrero, a high-crowned Mexican type, was also white with a band of rhinestones around it.

"Hope you get a thrill out of this," Jess went on, after shaking hands with Esther and Paula. "Our rodeos are similar, of course, but there is a difference, too."

"We're thrilled already and we haven't seen anything yet," Audrey replied eagerly. "We're hoping Monica wins the cup this year," she added quietly.

The Rodeo Queen nodded her head. "I hope so, too. She tries every year. I think it would give her a real interest in life, for she lives a lonely one. If she could just get a chance at doing work like this. She's a born trick rider, you know."

This conversation was held quite low and, although Esther and Paula heard it, Monica was much too busy trying to keep Jo-Jo in line to hear anything.

"I suppose you must be a winner at something before getting work like this to do?" Esther asked.

"Well, at least, some proof that you really can trick ride," the Rodeo Queen answered. "Monica is young, but it isn't a career that lasts long for your age tells."

"Then what are you left with?" Audrey asked wonderingly.

"Training other riders, of course," Jess replied.

"Just like her dad did. That's why she's so good."

"Now I'm getting some sense out of this," Audrey murmured, and Jess laughed.

"Anything is easy once you know it," she returned with a chuckle and then, turning her head at a warning shout, added. "Enjoy yourselves. I'd better get over to the front row. Cheerio, Canada!" and like a breath of home to the girls she rode off to the front.

Six cowgirls, in white riding breeches with blouses of red or blue, formed behind her and Audrey saw that the colours of the flag were being carried out. Monica touched her arm and motioned her forward behind the cowgirls.

"They are her ladies of the court," she explained. "We'll be right behind." She glanced back and waved to Esther and Paula to follow.

Suddenly a white truck backed into the dug-out right in front of the Rodeo Queen, and on it stood a ten-piece band. A silence! A warning fanfare and then the band struck up. A tall, straight-shouldered elderly man on another white horse rode behind the truck carrying the Flag.

The shouts of the crowds swelled to one tremendous roar as the truck and the Grand Marshal with his Flag, followed by the Rodeo Queen and her attendants, swept into the Arena. Audrey felt her throat go dry with excitement, while Monica grinned to the crowd. Once, Jo-Jo pranced sideways as if to leave the Parade and the crowd clapped. He bowed his head as if he had been applauded and Monica caught him back into the Parade.

Behind Esther and Paula rode cowboys in broad-brimmed hats, coiled ropes at saddle forks, and wearing shirts as colourful as their own. They waved their sombreros to the crowd, who were now making a noise that was almost deafening.

Round and round they went until everyone had seen them. Then the truck with the band swerved into the dug-out and disappeared. The Rodeo Queen and her court passed along to the judges' table and waited, while Monica showed the girls where to dismount and find their way back to Mr. Dean and Mr. Chapman.

The girls thanked the same tall girl again as they handed her the reins of their horses. She gave them more detailed instructions on how to get to the back of the grandstand so they could walk down to their own seats. They hurried off. They were so afraid that they would miss the first event that they stood waiting impatiently while a few late-comers got in their way, who were hunting for their seats.

"The fanfare hasn't sounded yet," Esther gasped, as she hung on to the arm of Audrey, who was now hurrying them along. "Couldn't we slow down to a gallop? I'm winded."

"Out of practice," Paula commented drily, as she loped along at their side. "Remember the good old schooldays when we used to beat the last bell by mere seconds?"

"I was lots younger then," Esther returned primly.

"That's right. I forgot that, Esther," Paula returned regretfully. Then looking at Audrey she winked. "We'll just have to give her a helping hand I'm afraid. Old age has got her."

"Oh, stop it, you two," Audrey laughed. "I haven't enough breath left to laugh."

"Another one," Paula moaned, and rushed past them as they made a grab for her.

So it was a breathless, laughing trio that finally made their way to Mr. Denton's side.

"Has it started yet?" Audrey gasped, taking off her sombrero and waving it to cool her face.

Mr. Denton shook his head. "No. They always make a slight delay, just for late-comers. I think it makes people enjoy the events all the more if they are kept waiting a little."

"It's good for us that they do have a delay," Esther returned, taking big gulps of air.

"Where does Monica come in?" Paula breathed.

Mr. Denton pointed to the dug-out and then showed them how the contestants would fan out, ready to begin their competition riding. The blare of a loud-speaker announcing the first event interrupted him and the show began.

The girls sat watching entranced as the rope spinners dashed out and began to do back flips with their ropes, dancing out and in the huge loops they were making. Mr. Denton explained that they were called butterfly and wedding-ring loops. Out and in, with the neatness and precision of machines, they danced until, with a loud applause, they bowed and departed. Next, saddle bronco-riding was announced. It was thrilling, of course, but Audrey felt jumpy and nervous at the bad spills some of the riders took, and was secretly a little glad when it was over. The babble of voices, punctuated by excited laughter, filled the air after this. Event after event went colourfully by and the girls waited impatiently for the trick riders to come on.

"Isn't it time for Monica's trick-riding yet?" Audrey asked at last.

Mr. Denton shook his head. "It's always the last on the program. The little folk are next. You'll get quite a kick out of them, for they work so hard to please and enjoy themselves as much as you do. Look! Here they come!"

He broke off and pointed and the girls laughed and clapped as little children, riding shaggy Shetland ponies all done up in red, white and blue ribbons, rode past waving to everyone.

"Aren't they sweet?" floated through the air. The murmur showed the crowd was clearly pleased. The children were just as pleased at the attention their fancy mounts were getting as they rode on, for they waved their tiny sombreros and laughed back at the crowd.

After the children had left the Arena, the trick-riding event was finally announced and the girls found they were absolutely limp from clapping. The silence that followed the fanfare was impressive and, when the first of the cowgirls rode out, the applause was deafening. Audrey counted ten riders. Esther picked out Monica right away.

"She rides that horse like she was part of it," she added.

The girls circled and waited. Then the first one rode off at a signal and shot round the Arena at a breathsnatching pace. Jumping off and on while the horse was galloping looked terribly dangerous, but the rider was taking it as if it was mere child's play. The next one seemed to be trying to fall off her horse, by the amount of times she kept slipping back, but it was all a trick to make the audience gasp. The next and the next went on and then, at last, it was Monica's turn.

The girls could see the sparkling blouse as Monica, with a twirl of her Stetson, started in a nice canter around the Arena. Slowly but surely she gained speed—then suddenly she slipped dexterously under

Jo-Jo's neck, settling herself on tightly with her knees and spreading out her arms under Jo-Jo's head to show she wasn't holding on. Audrey held her breath. The crowd went wild. Around and around she went in this precarious position while Jo-Jo put on more speed. Then, with precision neatness, Monica flipped round and came back up on his back.

When Jo-Jo came to where the girls were sitting, Monica slipped quickly off his back, making the crowd gasp, but she landed neatly on her feet while Jo-Jo, still quivering from his race, stopped instantly at her side. There they took their grand finale bow together. Jo-Jo bent his head down to the crowd and then pawed the ground with one hoof. This brought a roar of laughter. Bouncing on to his back again and waving to the girls, Monica rode off. Another silence reigned while everyone speculated on the results of the trick-riding contest.

A few minutes later, the crowd resumed its shouts of pleasure when the judge's voice began to announce the result over the loud-speaker system,

"The winner of the trick-riding in this year's Rodeo is Miss Monica Evans, who richly deserves this silver cup."

The girls looked at one another in keen delight. *Monica had won!*

A Shock for Monica

6

As THE BAND CAME BACK OUT AGAIN into the Arena and started to play, the girls, with Mr. Dean, Mr. Chapman and Mr. Denton hurried out of their seats toward the aisle. The Rodeo was over!

"We'll pick Monica up at the gate," Mr. Denton told them as they slowed up with the crowd, who were now pushing toward the main gate. "Her dad is going to stay to box up Jo-Jo and join us later."

"I'm glad Jo-Jo was all right," Esther whispered to Audrey.

Audrey nodded emphatically. "Me, too. The thought of Monica losing her pet horse, Jo-Jo, was unthinkable."

"She must have been mistaken about the Mexican, Pedro Lorenzo," Paula commented behind them. "When we hurried over to the dug-out I was almost afraid to look in case Jo-Jo had been spirited away before we got there."

"Jo-Jo is more than a horse to Monica," Audrey remarked, as they all stood outside the gates waiting. "He's a friend . . . a very dear friend."

"And he knows her so well," Esther laughed. "She only has to whistle lightly and he bounds over to her, ready for whatever she wants."

"She certainly has a lot of cool nerve to do what she did today," Paula remarked. "When she flew off Jo-Jo's back on to the ground I expected Jo-Jo to trample her."

"He knew she was going to do that trick and knew exactly what he was supposed to do," Audrey replied. "That's what makes them so good."

"The way she hung on underneath his nose like that gave me the horrors," Esther murmured. "Her face, as she went by us, was quite confident though."

"That's the difference between being well-trained and just knowing a little," Audrey returned. "Personally, I'll ride my horse right side up," she added with a chuckle.

"Me, too," Paula agreed. "The Rodeo Queen wasn't kidding when she said she was good."

"How thankful I am that she won, she'll. . . ." Audrey stopped when her dad caught her arm.

"Here she comes!" Mr. Dean called out and turning they saw Monica come hurrying over from the side door, still clasping her silver cup tightly in one hand. Several people stopped and congratulated her, which brought a rosy flush of embarrassment to her tanned face.

"Good for you," Mr. Dean laughed, shaking hands solemnly with her while the girls clustered round her, all trying to talk at once.

The silver cup was turned round and round for inspection while Mr. Denton nodded proudly.

"I knew you could do it, Monica," he said. "Always said it."

"Your dad will be so proud of you," Mr. Chapman murmured with a smile and then waved to a figure in the distance. "Here he comes now!"

They all turned to see Mr. Evans push through the crowd to them, his face crinkling up in an even brighter smile than usual. He patted his daughter on the back and laughed.

"Perfect timing, my dear. Couldn't find a fault anywhere," he declared warmly, and Monica's face glowed with the praise. Audrey knew that Monica's dad had given the highest praise you can give for a performance such as Monica's. No wonder she looked so contented.

It was a breathlessly happy Monica surrounded by her new Canadian friends that finally made their way back to the hotel. There they found to their astonishment, that the management was preparing a quiet celebration dinner for the winners of the various events. The girls could hardly wait for the evening to come, for everyone had been told to come in cowboy outfits, even the guests in the hotel had to plan their outfits to fit the occasion also.

By the time the girls, with the four men, had made their cautious way into the dining room later, the whole room seemed to be literally thronged with sombreros, glistening belts and colourful outfits.

"All we need now is Billy the Kid to make his appearance," Audrey chuckled, as they made their way to their own table.

Suddenly the murmur of voices dwindled to silence as a huge man in a black shirt with the shiny badge of SHERIFF on it, stood up.

"Ladies and Gentlemen," he began. "I know that all of you were at the Rodeo today and saw some of the best and cleverest tricks done on horseback that you could wish to see." He grinned. "Why, some of those tricks I don't believe I could do myself," he added with a drawl that set everyone laughing, for the thought of such a big man trying such fancy tricks on a horse was funny. "But seriously now, I do want to say that I'm real proud to congratulate these winners myself tonight and to thank all of the others for trying. I know that our friend, Mayor Russell of our fine city of Redmond, would like to meet these winners personally, so I have asked for these winners to be present tonight and to come forward now."

Audrey grinned at Monica when an announcer called out the winners of the various events and she rose to go.

"You're a celebrity, remember," she whispered and Monica giggled.

Several times during that dinner Audrey saw Mr. Evans slip away and then return. She wondered at it and caught Monica's eyes following her dad as he came back in again for the third time. They exchanged looks and Mr. Evans nodded. Monica turned and smiled to Audrey.

"Dad is keeping an eye out for Jo-Jo," she whispered. "This is the time for any horse thieving to be done."

"I thought that danger was all over now," Paula gasped farther over.

"So did I," Esther whispered at her other side. "I thought they would have had their chance before the Rodeo began."

Monica shook her head. "No. The Grounds are watched very carefully before the Rodeo but they slacken off after it's all over."

After the dinner, some entertainment had been planned with cowboy singing and guitar playing. Everyone was invited to join in the songs and the girls thoroughly enjoyed this for they knew most of them, as both Canada and the U.S. use nearly all the same ones. The time really flew after that and it was with some regret that they rose to go. But it was a tired and happy foursome that finally made their sleepy way upstairs to lie and talk it over for a little while longer.

In the morning, they were all up bright and early as they had planned to get home before the sun was at its hottest. Breakfast quickly taken, they were soon back upstairs getting ready for their return journey home. The hotel was emptying quickly as if the other guests had had the same idea.

Mr. Denton had been missing all morning and Audrey's curiosity had finally got the best of her as the four came back downstairs.

"Isn't Mr. Denton coming home with us?" she inquired of Monica, who nodded.

"Yes. I was wondering where he was myself, though," she admitted. "I asked Dad but he doesn't know either."

"Probably met someone he knows," Esther put in, and that sounded probable to the others.

Mr. Evans and Mr. Chapman were talking in the hall of the hotel when Mr. Denton came hurrying in and over to them, a bright beaming smile on his face. He waved to the girls sitting in the huge armchairs in the lounge, and they got up eagerly and came over. Mr. Dean was already paying the bill at the desk and then he, too, joined them.

"Well, let's get home," Mr. Denton chuckled. "It's just about the most perfect day we've had yet." He seemed very pleased about something.

And how true he was about the day. As they all filed out of the hotel door and gazed around them, they could feel the cool breeze fan their faces while the warm sun beat lightly down on their heads. Just the kind of perfect day you get when you're going home, Audrey thought ruefully. They turned toward the

48

stables at the back to pick up their horses, while Mr. Evans dashed away to get Jo-Jo's truck.

It was at the stable that Mr. Denton told them his good news. The girls had already mounted and were waiting for the men to go to the garage and get the car, when Mr. Denton spoke.

"Well, folks, I've just had the most wonderful offer for Jo-Jo . . . and I think I'll probably take it," he beamed, his eyes sparkling at the thought of the really wonderful price he had been offered.

In his elation he didn't notice that the four girls had stopped their chattering and were now looking down at him with shocked faces. Audrey looked quickly over at Monica and saw that even her tanned complexion had turned white.

"Some circus want him?" Mr. Dean asked, looking quickly at the girls.

Mr. Denton shook his head with a laugh. "No. One of the Rodeos that spend their time on the road putting on shows. They need the finest and best of trick horses . . . and they'll certainly get the finest and best when they get Jo-Jo," he added proudly. "Monica and her dad have worked hard with that horse, and Monica's horsemanship today showed off the cleverness of both horse and rider. Jo-Jo knew everything Monica wanted him to do. Yes, sir. A marvellous piece of business."

As he turned and walked toward the garage that was farther over from the stable, Mr. Dean and Mr. Chapman glanced sympathetically up at Monica. They had been quick to feel the sudden change in the atmosphere and had guessed, but Mr. Denton in his excitement hadn't even noticed.

The journey home was the most painful that Audrey

had ever endured on horseback. A glance at Monica's white face filled her with a great longing to be able to do something. But what could she do? Jo-Jo was Mr. Denton's horse. He had the right to sell him if he wanted to. Esther and Paula had remained quietly in the background. They felt that silence was the best thing at the moment.

When Mr. Evans drove the truck out of the gate and got in front of them, Audrey felt she couldn't bear it any more. Monica's face had gone set and, if possible, had turned a shade whiter when the horse truck slid in in front of them. They could just see the top of Jo-Jo's head.

"Maybe Mr. Denton will change his mind, Monica," Audrey whispered.

Monica turned and looked at her sadly. "Jo-Jo belongs to him. I know he'll get me another horse and that Dad will help me train him, but . . . it won't be Jo-Jo," the last words were choked off and sounded so heartbroken that Audrey felt a quick rush of tears. What a horrible ending to such a good time. She felt as if her whole trip to California had been ruined.

"Couldn't you tell him that you didn't want another horse?" Audrey ventured, after another unhappy pause.

Monica shook her head. "It would seem ungrateful for all he has done for Dad and I. He gave my dad a good job even though he wasn't as well experienced as most ranch managers are, and he's helped to put me through High School. So you see, I couldn't."

"I believe he wouldn't consider the sale if he knew how you really felt, Monica," Audrey insisted.

"Maybe. But that wouldn't be fair to him. It's his horse and horses are his business. He often sells his thoroughbreds and . . ."

"But Jo-Jo is special," Audrey interrupted fiercely.

"I know," Monica replied wearily. "That's why he got such a good offer for him."

Audrey glanced back at her chums riding solemnly together and caught their sympathetic eyes watching Monica. She sighed. What could three girls do about the situation anyway? She suddenly smiled as a thought struck her. She had prayed earnestly that night for Monica to have her desire in winning the silver cup—well, why couldn't she take this present trouble to the very same Heavenly Father to take care of in His Own way?

"I sure wish there was something we could do for you, Monica," Audrey remarked, after another long painful pause. "But, what can we do?"

Monica turned and looked at her and Audrey saw the tears glittering in her eyes. She tried to smile.

"Just having you kids here has helped more than you'll ever know," she said quietly. "It doesn't make me feel so alone," she added, her voice breaking.

"You're never alone, Monica . . . remember?" Audrey said softly.

Monica shook her head. "It's easy for you to say that . . . you're sure."

"You could be, too," Audrey replied. She sighed, as she looked once more at the truck ahead. "If only you would try and see it our way."

"I'm not trying to be stubborn . . . but . . . I just can't see it, somehow," Monica returned jerkily, as she tried valiantly to stem the tears that would insist on flowing.

"Maybe you're not trying very hard to see, Monica," Audrey replied quietly.

"What do you mean?" Monica's voice was sharp.

"You just say, 'I just can't see it' and you don't ask God for help."

Monica sighed. "I'll try," she murmured, and stared fixedly ahead at the moving truck. Audrey knew that the conversation was now closed.

She was glad when they finally dipped into the roadway that led to Little Creek Ranch. Mr. Evans drove the truck toward the corral and the girls rode to the stables. When Mr. Denton had parked the car they could still hear him talking brightly about the offer. The girls turned sorrowfully toward the ranch-house where Mrs. Denton stood waiting for them with a puzzled look on her face at their quietness.

Audrey tried to smile as she saw her and Monica even called out a listless "Hi!" but that was as far as they could go. They turned as they crowded on to the porch and looked back at the truck. Mr. Evans was now opening the runway down for Jo-Jo to disembark. They watched as he swung the big double doors open and the horse, with its shining saddle, proudly descended to the yard. Audrey's eyes filled with tears as Monica suddenly stepped down and whistled lightly.

Suddenly Audrey dashed the tears from her eyes in fright when Monica's horrified voice split the silent air.

"Dad! That isn't Jo-Jo you've got there!"

The Gospel Message

7

FOR ONE MINUTE EVERYONE STOOD paralysed by Monica's hoarse shout and then the men, shaking off their surprise, dashed over to the horse. Mr. Evans, who had been shutting the big double doors, came running down the runway while the girls flew off the porch.

Audrey, Esther and Paula looked bewildered at the horse for, to them, it was the same one they had seen in the yard and at the Rodeo. But Monica was shaking her head.

"I thought he looked different. That was why I whistled," she told them all. "He has about the same markings as Jo-Jo, but that's all."

"These Palominos all look the same to me," Mr. Dean replied bewildered.

"They're bred for their colour, so it's not surprising that they all look alike," Mr. Denton replied absent-mindedly. He sighed and turned toward the ranch house. "Well, I guess I better call the Sheriff about this."

"Pedro Lorenzo was in town after all," Audrey remarked to Monica and Mr. Denton, who had started to walk away, spun around at her voice.

"*Who* was in town?"

Audrey swallowed nervously at his fierce tone, but Monica explained for her.

Monica's dad took over when Monica had finished. "I didn't think the scare was big enough to worry you about," he said. "I thought I had him well protected. There was always someone with him . . . I saw to that."

Mr. Denton patted him on the shoulder. "Even if you had told me I probably would have thought Monica was mistaken . . . so don't reproach yourself."

"It might not have been Pedro Lorenzo who took him," Mr. Dean put in hopefully. "That might have been just a coincidence."

"It might be. But knowing Pedro Lorenzo I'm not so sure," Mr. Evans replied gloomily.

"I realise Jo-Jo has gone, but I still can't see Pedro getting away with him," Mr. Denton said. "I'll tell the Sheriff anyway. It might give him a lead."

"Going to be one tricky job trying to find one particular Palomino when this part of the country breeds them," Mr. Evans muttered, as he stood patting the head of the strange horse. "One of the men I hired at the Grounds must have been working with the horsethief," he added with a groan.

"Then he must have been taken for his clever training," Mr. Chapman put in.

"Absolutely," Mr. Evans agreed. "No finer trick horse in this country."

It was after lunch, which was a gloomy affair, when the girls had got together again on the porch, that Audrey made a suggestion to Monica.

"Couldn't we ride back to the Rodeo Grounds and see if we can pick up some clue to Jo-Jo's disappearance?"

Monica frowned thoughtfully. "The Sheriff will be there doing that now," she replied tonelessly. The shock of hearing of Jo-Jo's probable sale and now its disappearance had taken the heart completely out of her. Her woebegone expression had strengthened the resolve of the three Canadians to do their best to help, if only to keep her from brooding.

"But nobody knows Jo-Jo like you do," Esther took it up hopefully. "The Sheriff only saw him performing at the Rodeo, while you've taken care of him and . . ." she floundered to a stop.

"No harm in trying," Paula finished.

Monica shrugged. "I suppose we could try. Let's go then!" She walked slowly away with the others trailing behind her. They weren't sure whether this was a good idea or not, but it might help Monica's state of mind if they kept her busy.

As they neared the Rodeo Grounds a little later, they felt rather dispirited for the sun was now pouring down on them making the heat almost unbearable. The dust was rising again and choking them, but they kept doggedly at it until the Grounds came in view.

The town was slowly emptying of its Rodeo visitors and only the locals remained talking over the events as the girls finally cantered in through the big front gate and over to where Mr. Evans had parked Jo-Jo's truck.

Dismounting and tying their horses, the four girls walked round the now empty place without much hope. The Grounds looked as empty as a prairie. By the amount of footprints they found, apparently the Sheriff had already been there.

"There are several hoofprints but that could be some of the strange horse's prints, too," Monica said wearily. "There was nothing outstanding about Jo-Jo's that I know of."

"Don't give up, Monica," Audrey said in a pleading tone of voice and the Californian girl tried to smile, but it was a poor attempt.

"Probably Jo-Jo is across the Border by now," Esther said worriedly, but Monica shook her head.

"They won't make it tonight," she replied. "They'll probably camp somewhere and then try again Monday night."

"Why Monday night?" Paula asked suddenly. "Why not tomorrow through the day when they can see better?"

"Nothing passes over the Border on Sunday, which is tomorrow, and they would be picked up instantly."

They stayed around for half an hour longer but nothing more could they pick up. Monica's tearful face wrung the hearts of her new friends, for they felt so helpless to do anything. The journey back was even longer than the first time to Audrey, for now their first faint hope of finding a clue was gone.

When they reached the ranch house again they found that the Sheriff had just been there to get all the details, and was now going back over the old ground where Pedro Lorenzo had been picked up before. There was nothing more for the girls to do but wait.

On Sunday after breakfast, Audrey asked Mrs. Denton if there was a church nearby. She nodded quickly.

"Oh, yes. It isn't really a church," she amended apologetically. "It really is just a hall that is used for the country folk for their services on Sunday. Rev. Keith Randall is good, even if he is young."

While Audrey and Mrs. Denton had been discussing the service, Audrey had caught Monica's startled expression. Esther and Paula were asked quick questions now and Audrey turned and looked over at Monica.

"Is it possible to get there today?"

Monica swallowed uncomfortably. "Mr. Denton might take us." The answer was rather hesitant and Audrey knew she wasn't sure how to handle the situation.

"Of course my husband will take you," Mrs. Denton put in quickly. "Monica used to go to Sunday School there all the time. She isn't as regular to church as she ought to be."

Monica flushed under the slightly disapproving tone. "Well . . . I'd like to go today," she said slowly, as the others looked at her.

Audrey smiled inwardly. Had the shock of losing her pet, after learning he might be sold, brought Monica to realise how inadequate she was to handle her own life? Strange, how people went sailing along without once thinking about their Heavenly Father, and then suddenly get a mental shock that made them start wondering about Him.

She sighed. It wasn't the way she had planned to have Monica want her Heavenly Father, but perhaps her way wouldn't have been the right way. She smiled over to her.

"It would make our vacation just perfect," and Monica smiled back.

Mr. Denton was quite eager to take them. "I go to the evening service myself because I can't get away in the morning," he explained, before hurrying away to get the car.

In a few minutes, the girls, with Mr. Chapman and Mr. Dean in the front seat with Mr. Denton, were gliding quickly out of the yard and on to the highway.

San Paloma seemed deserted when they entered. The shops being shut and everyone gone, made it look like a ghost town. The hall, Mr. Denton explained, was at the very end of the long street.

57

"Most folks go into San Diego to the big churches, but Mr. Randall comes out here for the folks that can't take such a trip," he explained.

Audrey and the others glanced interestingly round as the car stopped in front of a one-storey wooden building that was painted white. Its door stood invitingly open and Audrey saw that a few people were walking slowly up the steep stairs and disappearing inside.

The hall itself was plain with wooden seats that creaked slightly when you sat on them, and at the farthest end was a small dais with an upright piano at one side of it. A few arrangements had been made to make the service possible for Mr. Randall, and their addition helped. The seats were partially filled now with more people still coming in, and Audrey was surprised to find that so many had already come. They looked hot and dusty as if they had walked all the way. She nodded to a few who smiled over to her.

A young lad handed out hymnbooks and Audrey, glancing at the dais, saw the hymns numbers marked up at the side of the wall. Just as she had found the place, a young man appeared from the side of the dais and walked forward with a smile on his face. He was younger than Audrey had expected. The slight murmuring that had been going on stopped instantly and silence reigned.

Audrey noticed that Monica sang listlessly and looked broodingly out of the window, which was open and quite near her. It was certain that Monica's mind wasn't on spiritual things, Audrey reflected sadly, and turned to listen to Mr. Randall who had already started to speak.

"Lots of us think that by 'doing the best we can' that we are being Christians," he was saying, and

Audrey felt a shock of surprise go through her, for those were the exact words Monica had used when she had asked her if she was a Christian. Monica had straightened up, too, and her dark eyes widened in amazement.

"The first thing we should ask ourselves is . . . 'Do I keep the Lord's Commandments?' Take the first and greatest commandment. 'Thou shalt love the Lord thy God with all thy heart, and with all thy soul, and with all thy mind.' Do we do that when we just take Him for granted without doing anything more about it?" The young man paused and Audrey heard Monica draw in a sharp breath.

"Of course not, and yet, by not obeying that commandment we have committed the greatest sin of all. According to God's standards we are lost."

Audrey saw with delight that Monica was really listening now, a slight frown of concentration on her brow.

"Lots of us ask if it was necessary for Jesus to die. Have you wondered, too?" He smiled as he asked the question. "Well, reason it out. We had broken God's law; the penalty was death. Now what other way could that penalty be paid other than by death?" He looked fixedly at them as if to impress them by what he said next. "But God so loved us that He didn't want us to die, to be separated from Him forever. Remember that would have been forever," he repeated firmly. "But He sent His beloved Son, Jesus, to die as our substitute and pay our penalty for us which was death."

Monica turned and caught Audrey's glance. Her face looked thoughtful, and Audrey winged a prayer that it was bringing her nearer to understanding.

"Surely there is no one here who would reject such a Saviour?" Mr. Randall shook his head. "No one could possibly reject such a love that led our Redeemer to die for him on Calvary's cross! And yet there are so many who don't believe, or don't want to believe, simply because things are not working out for them as they had hoped. And still others, who do believe, but feel that that is all that is necessary for them to do. In other words, they take that great sacrifice as if it was nothing—remember Our Saviour had to endure trials, and not for Himself either, but for us who so easily forget Him or take Him for granted.

"What more wonderful source of comfort do we have than our Heavenly Father? We have our parents to go to comfort us, I know. But sometimes even they can't take away the worry and trouble that besets us. Remember that God has never at any time forsaken anyone. We have but to pray, to call upon Him at any time, and He will answer us. By faith we know that and faith is logical. It is not something you work into or for. It is a gift, and you can thank that same God for it. You use that faith to let God accomplish things in you, for you, and through you.

"The only way you can be a true witness for your Lord Jesus Christ is to make that faith the basis for living victoriously over sin and evil. Others will be quick enough to see it in your life, and follow."

Audrey had become so engrossed that she had forgotten Monica for a moment. But turning suddenly she saw a rapt expression on her face that gladdened her. Mr. Randall couldn't have picked a better sermon for their new friend—her thoughts snapped off as the young minister's voice caught her attention again.

"Why not take the Saviour as your own? Be born

again. Remember, that by letting Jesus into your heart to cleanse it from wickedness you have the assurance of Someone, who is always near, to protect and guide you as a Father."

Audrey drew in a deep breath as the young minister announced the last hymn. Had Monica really got something out of this morning's service? She glanced at her again and saw her flicking the pages of her hymnbook with a thoughtful air.

Back in the car again, silence held each one as if they were still digesting Mr. Randall's sermon. Audrey was content to watch the varying thoughts flicker across Monica's expressive face, and hope.

"Mr. Randall was wonderful, I think," Paula declared stoutly, as the four girls put away their hats and coats in their bedroom.

"Yes, he was," Monica answered quietly, and the other three glanced at one another. "I never thought of God in such a personal way before . . . it sounds so wonderful," her voice dropped to a whisper, but that was all she said and for a moment Audrey felt a twinge of disappointment. Then she remembered something that her mother used to tell her.

"Once the seed is sown, all you can do is to wait and pray hard."

Audrey mentally agreed and knew that she would definitely pray harder than ever for Monica, who really wanted to be a Christian, but was still too uncertain of what it meant to really be one.

On a Clue Hunt

8   ON MONDAY MORNING, MONICA WAS roving restlessly around the house looking out of one window and then another. Audrey knew she was watching for the Sheriff to appear with some good news, but as the morning went slowly by and no Sheriff appeared, Monica's face grew graver.

"I suppose Jo-Jo will be in Mexico by now," Paula remarked sadly, but Monica shook her head.

"Not till night time. They wouldn't take the chance of trying to cross the Border in broad daylight."

"Oh, that's right," Paula replied. "I asked that before. They naturally wouldn't want to be seen."

Suddenly Audrey had another inspiration. "You know, Monica, I think I know which way they have taken Jo-Jo." Monica didn't say anything but just waited. "Remember I told you when we were on the train that we saw the Mexicans ride past us?" Monica nodded. "Well, if we went back that way couldn't we find their trail and get the Sheriff on to it?"

"But if they came across the desert how could we find their trail?" Monica asked with a frown. Then she asked suddenly. "Did they come directly across or just down the side?"

Audrey shook her head. "I'm not sure, Monica. We saw some American cowboys pass first and . . ."

"Which direction?"

Monica's quick question startled Audrey. She

thought. "The same direction as the Mexicans . . . whatever that direction was," she added lamely. "I'm sorry I couldn't say."

"They must have come from Hollywood . . . the American cowboys, I mean," Monica replied briskly. "They were probably extras doing some picture work. So that might mean the Mexicans were doing the same thing." She seemed to be talking more to herself than the girls, but they didn't interrupt her train of thought. "So . . . they could have gone up on the hills instead of across the desert . . ." she broke off. "Could you show me if we went back there now?"

They were all sure they could, and in a whirl of eagerness they hurried out to their horses. Soon they were flying back along the way they had been, and then Audrey took her to where they had seen the riders from the train. Forgotten was the discomfort of the broiling sun overhead. They now had something definite they could look for.

Audrey groaned as they finally went into the deep parts of the dusty stretch. It had looked bad enough from the train, but actually riding out on it was past describing. Monica rode purposely forward seemingly unaware of the heat, while the other three followed gamely. They had had many hard rides themselves in the Canadian hills and weren't going to be beaten by a long stretch of dusty waste in California. On and on they flew while Audrey gave directions to Monica beside her.

As they neared the place where they had first seen the Mexicans, Monica reined her horse and the others stopped beside her.

"Now which way?" she asked.

"I would say over there," Audrey replied, pointing

toward the hills. "I know it wasn't across all that stretch of sand." She shuddered as she again beheld that lonely picture of desert.

"Then we'll take this cut-off," Monica replied and whirled to the right. "It'll be cooler up here," she added, and the three behind her fervently hoped so.

It seemed hours later to them that Monica finally began to slowly climb the brown-earthed hill, its ascent so gradual that you nearly missed it. The trees were thick and looked invitingly cool, and the four coaxed their mounts to keep moving.

Farther up, Monica again stopped and slid from her horse. The others waited. Had she found something? They watched her curiously as she poked around the broad path and toward the edges.

"Find anything?" Audrey called out, and jumped when her voice bore down on her again. "Some echo," she laughed nervously.

Monica came round to her. "There are four distinct hoofprints, but whether they are the ones we're looking for, I don't know." She smiled. "We'd feel silly to bring the Sheriff up this far just for nothing."

"We can try farther up," Esther suggested.

"Why not walk up and leave the horses tied?" Paula asked. "Did you notice the echo Audrey's voice made just now? They'll hear our horses a mile away."

"Good idea, Paula," Monica approved, and immediately tied her horse on a clearing farther up. The others followed her.

Walking was much easier than riding on such a crooked path, and the girls had done quite a stretch before Audrey glanced at her watch and gasped.

"Do you know it's past our tea-time, Monica?" she

asked. "Mrs. Denton will wonder what has happened to us."

Monica nodded. "We'd better get back," she agreed hurriedly. "I guess we were wrong to think that they came up this way," she added, glancing around her at the thick foliage and immense trees that surrounded them.

"Well, it was a try anyway," Audrey cheered, turning round and walking back again. "I hope you know where we are," she added with a laugh, "I'd hate to get lost up here."

Monica smiled. "I know where we are, Audrey. Don't worry."

It was quite dark where they were for the over-hanging branches of the trees completely hid the sun, which was now descending in the West. The air had sprung up cool and sharp and they shivered slightly, although they were again in their gay cowgirl outfits.

"I'm glad we have these heavy clothes on, although I do wish I had worn a jacket," Audrey mourned.

"We'll be home in no time," Monica cheered.

"How could it get so cold so quickly," Paula grumbled.

"The sun has blotted completely out so there may be a storm coming up," Monica replied, and the slight worry in her voice brought Audrey's heart to her throat. She had been told of these quick Western storms and didn't want to experience one up in the forest here. Without another word the four started to run, but after a few collisions with unseen objects, they decided to take their time and get there un-scratched.

How far away were they from home? They had kept on walking, keeping the tracks on the ground well in sight. Even now they could still see them. It might have been other cowboys that had ridden up here, although Audrey had a strange feeling that it was the Mexicans. If they had only been able to find them without their knowing it and then get hold of the Sheriff.

One point in the forest showed the sky overhead, and Audrey's fears mounted again when she saw the dark mass of fluffy clouds. She peered at Monica and saw her grim expression. It was a storm coming up! How stupid of them to go so far away.

"The horses must be round the next bend," Monica said suddenly and Audrey gave a sigh of relief.

The girls unconsciously walked a little faster and scurried round the bend with a hopeful look in their eyes. There, to their delight, were the horses stamping impatiently as if they were annoyed at being tied when a storm was due.

Audrey opened her mouth to say something funny when the words froze on her lips. For, as they looked, the bushes at the side parted and the three Mexican cowboys, that they had seen before, stepped forward with evil leers on their faces and stood waiting beside the horses.

Prisoners

9

"WE WAIT, SEÑORITA," ONE OF THE Mexicans drawled silkily, and stepped forward. By the dim light of the twilight, Audrey recognised the one Monica had called Pedro Lorenzo.

"What for?" Monica asked bluntly and walked straight toward her horse. But she spun around sharply when a coil of rope whirled over her head, pinning her arms to her sides. A handkerchief gag was thrust roughly into her mouth.

At sight of this, Audrey dashed to the side of the road where blackness lay at its thickest and cowered behind some of the foliage, but already another of the Mexicans had followed swiftly. She felt the coarse rope bite through the sleeves of her satin blouse. Making her walk in front of him, Audrey turned and saw Esther and Paula in a similar predicament. She felt furious at herself for mentioning the idea of hunting for the Mexicans. If she had only kept her mouth shut, they wouldn't be here.

Lifting them easily on to their horses the girls were forced to follow Pedro, who was taking the reins of Monica's horse and leading him up the hill. Audrey tried to avoid the gag that the tall, lean Mexican was pushing into her face but it was no use. In a moment, she, too, couldn't speak.

Only Esther had been able to escape the gags and she let out scream after scream that echoed up and down the hills and made icy worms of fear coast down

Audrey's spine. But in a second she was silenced. The men had not said one word after Pedro's greeting to Monica. Audrey peered down at the man walking beside her horse, but she couldn't make out anything but a rough head of black hair.

They walked back up the path the girls had been on, when Pedro suddenly halted. Leaving the reins in the hands of the third Mexican, he walked into the darkness. The girls peered after him but it was a few minutes before he returned leading three more horses, their own apparently.

"Move up, Lopez!" Pedro's snap command brought the Mexican who was beside Audrey, hurrying forward. There, a whispered conversation went on with the three. A few minutes later Lopez returned to Audrey's side, pulling her horse forward in line with Monica's, while the third Mexican brought Paula and Esther in line with each other now. Pedro, on horseback, was in the lead again. The other two Mexicans dropped behind the girls. With such an arrangement it would be impossible for any of them to make their escape.

Audrey glanced quickly at Monica but their new friend was sitting quiet, her eyes staring straight ahead. As if feeling Audrey's eyes on her, she turned and nodded. It was her only means of greeting.

The party had proceeded but a short way again when Pedro again halted and came round to Monica's side, removing her gag.

"Why deed you come up here, señorita?" he asked, and the oiliness in his voice made Audrey's heart beat a little faster. These Mexicans were worried. They were wondering how much they knew. Then suddenly she guessed why they had been captured. If the echo was as good as it had been when she spoke, then the

Mexicans must have heard her, too, and no doubt had thought that the four of them had overheard them making their plans farther up. It was the only explanation.

"I didn't know there was a law against riding up here," Monica drawled.

Pedro hesitated for a minute. Audrey knew he would like to have believed Monica's innocent tone of voice, but he daren't take the chance. Horse stealing was still a Federal offence.

Pedro turned away without replacing the gag. Monica spoke again.

"How about taking the gags out of my friends' mouths, too . . . they won't yell." Her rather high, derisive tone brought Pedro's glowering face in view again.

"W-e-ll . . . eet would do no good to yell up here," he laughed coarsely and removed Audrey's gag. The men in the rear, seeing their boss's actions, did the same to Paula and Esther. Audrey sighed in relief.

The sullen leader rode forward again and the party moved on. The sky had steadily grown blacker until now nothing could be seen. The path was still wide enough to let two horses abreast go by, but the trees and bushes at the side looked threatening. Suddenly a vivid flash of lightning, a crack of thunder, and the deluge that Monica had spoken of earlier, really began.

A heavy blanket was laid roughly over Audrey's shoulders and, peering from under it, she saw that the others had received the same. They were rather scratchy to the touch, but at least they helped to keep out a great deal of the rain that was now descending in sheets.

She groaned. So this was the freak rainstorms of

California. What a lovely place to experience your first one, she reflected wryly.

"I wonder if they'll take us over the Border with them?"

Monica's close whisper aroused Audrey from her gloomy reflections.

"What good would that do?" she whispered back, but Monica just shook her head warningly when Pedro turned his head slightly.

Audrey tugged at her wrists and tried to ease her shoulders from the noose they were in, but it was no use. These men had done a good neat job of tying them. The three men did not mind the storm, apparently, for the two in the rear were chattering in Spanish and laughing.

"This rain will blot out our trail," Monica said suddenly, and Audrey knew then why they were laughing.

As they descended down the hill on the other side, Audrey saw that there was a little hollow at one spot. She was staring hard at it, trying to see how deep it was, when suddenly Monica, without warning of any kind, fell sideways from her horse.

With an exclamation of anger, Pedro slipped from his horse and strode over to her. Picking her up lightly, he tossed her back on to her horse.

"Stay there!" he growled viciously.

"How can I ride when my hands are tied?" she snapped, sliding sideways again.

Pedro hesitated and then, fearing a trick of some sort, rode on. Audrey groaned inwardly. It had been a good try. She would try the trick herself, given an opportunity. The rain fell in torrents and showed no signs of stopping, and the seven riders were forced to go slowly. It was getting difficult for Pedro to find the trail and Audrey saw Monica grin over to her. So many times did they twist in and out amongst the trees on their fearful journey, that Audrey lost all sense of direction.

"If only we could do something," she said inaudibly and then, as her horse jogged over a rough place in the path, she deliberately slid from the saddle. Monica, catching sight of Audrey's fall, performed the same trick. Pedro hurried forward but didn't know which girl to go to first.

"Lopez!" he growled. "Get that . . ." he didn't finish as Paula and Esther, taking the cue from the other two girls, slid off sideways, too.

Pedro was furious. "Lopez! Chico! Get them back up!" he ordered. Getting off his own horse, he stepped over to Monica and pointed. "You try eet again and . . ." he didn't finish but the scowling, threatening face so close to her own made Monica jerk herself away.

"I can't ride with my hands tied," she repeated stubbornly, and then smiled when Pedro hesitated. With a gesture of impatience he cut the cord which held her wrists and arms. A signal to the other two men and all four girls were free. "I warn you," Pedro muttered angrily. "Try sometheeng and eet be better you hadn't."

On they rode once more but Audrey had to admit that, though they were still captive, it gave her a feeling that there might be a chance of escape if they weren't tied up.

The seven now rode in deep silence and it seemed to Audrey that they must have been riding for hours. She was beginning to feel faint with weariness and saw that even Monica was slumped down on the saddle. The storm showed no signs of abating, but rather increased. The trees that had been sheltering them a little were now straggling out to just a few here and there, until soon they were on the edge of the timber. It made harder going now, for the riders and Audrey knew that they either had to halt or try to battle the elements, which seemed nearly impossible to her.

Suddenly Pedro gave the signal again to stop and called to his companions. Audrey could not hear everything that was said, but any chance word she did get didn't help much for it was in Spanish. She glanced at Monica, who was straining forward listening. She crept nearer Audrey.

"They're going to stop somewhere," she whispered.

"Where?" Audrey gasped. In this driving rain nothing was visible either above or below. She saw Monica shrug, so, apparently, she didn't know either.

Audrey watched the men closely and saw that an argument was starting up. The rain was beating down hard on them but the flow of conversation didn't lessen. Pedro's excited voice seemed to get higher, and once he raised his arm threateningly. Monica glanced over and shrugged her shoulders.

"The other two don't like Pedro's plan," she whispered. "They're afraid."

"Not half as afraid as I am," Audrey muttered.

Lopez signalled Pedro that his voice was too loud and, after a quick, leering glance at the girls, Pedro lowered his voice.

"Now I can't hear a thing," Monica grumbled, and moved away as Pedro turned and glared at her.

"I hope they know where they are," Audrey whispered.

"I hope so, too," Monica sighed. "I'm hopelessly lost myself now."

"I'm cold . . . why can't they get moving," a voice whispered behind Monica, nearly unseating her. She turned and found Paula getting as near as she could.

"I'm hungry," Esther grumbled farther over, and her voice, being pitched higher than the others, brought the attention of the men.

"Quiet!" Pedro rasped out, and Paula crept back again.

Audrey sighed and took a deep breath. Her back and shoulders were killing her. How much longer could this go on?

Again the men returned giving the girls vicious looks as they passed them. They had their plans made up. Riding was so difficult now that Audrey felt she couldn't take it any more. The blanket kept slipping off her shoulders until her arms felt to breaking point grabbing for it. She could hear Monica taking deep breaths as the wind howled and bit into their faces. Would this never end? They must be nearly at the Border by now. Glancing up at the pitch-black sky, Audrey suddenly remembered her Heavenly Father and smiled. They weren't alone really. This may be just a test of her own faith in Him.

They hadn't gone very far when they approached a small clearing and, ahead of them, the girls saw a curious dark shadow nestled in amongst some trees farther ahead. Huge rocks were nearby it and, by peering forward, Audrey could just make out an old building of some sort. She glanced at Monica who caught it.

"An old disused monastery," she whispered and slid back when Chico reminded her with a push.

As they rode up nearer, they could see that it was

in a state of decayed ruin and was surmounted by a tower which, in olden times, had evidently been used as a look-out over the valley. It was not the austere building but the tower which attracted the girls. They knew without asking that they were to be imprisoned in it. For how long? That was the question uppermost in their minds as they were yanked off their horses and forced roughly inside the door of the old stone building. The heavy door clanged shut behind them.

They didn't resist when they were half dragged up a winding set of stairs to the tower, for they knew only worse treatment would be given them. When they reached the top of the stairs, they were thrust through another small door and into a tiny circular tower room. It was dingy and dark but Lopez, as if prepared, lit a candle and thrust it into a dirty bottle on a wooden table. It showed the girls that only one small window was overhead and too small to crawl through, while heavy iron bars kept any chance help from getting in, either. Cobwebs hung everywhere, making the girls cluster closer together in disgust. On one side stood a large cot with clean bed clothing upon it, and on the table beside the candle was now visible a wash basin and a cracked pitcher of water.

The girls glanced at each other and then spun around when the grating sound of a drawn bolt behind them told them that they were now alone in the tower room as prisoners.

A Ray of Hope

10   "WELL, ISN'T THIS CHEERY," AUDREY groaned, sitting down on the side of the bed with an exhausted sigh. "Where do we go from here, my hearty?" Her question was levelled at Monica, who shook her head.

"That's what I would like to know," she muttered, coming over and sitting down beside her. "Why have we been brought here?" Audrey gave her idea of why the Mexicans had been afraid to take the chance of leaving them behind. Monica nodded. "That's as good a reason as any, all right," she agreed. "I wish we had heard them."

Paula and Esther were now crouching at their feet on the floor, while the sputtering of the candle cast flickering dark shadows over the grey rough walls. Its soft plopping sound increased the quietness of the girls as they sat trying to rest their weary muscles from their hard ride. Suddenly Monica got up and hurried over to the door. Pressing her ear to the join of the door and wall she listened. The others held their breaths and waited. A few minutes later she returned to the edge of the bed in disgust.

"They're talking too low for me to hear anything," she reported.

"I wonder what they plan to do with us," Audrey said thoughtfully. Now that she was off her horse, weariness was really seeping through her and making concentration on their predicament difficult.

"Take us over the Border with them and then lose

us," Monica returned quickly. "They wouldn't hurt us . . . I don't think," she added thoughtfully. "Horse thieving is just about their stretch in crime."

"I'm starving," Paula moaned. "I wonder if this is going to be a starvation prison?"

"I hardly think so," Monica replied. "What would they gain by starving us?"

"Oh, for some chicken and dumplings," Esther moaned gently.

"Don't torture us, Esther," Audrey chided. "Remember! We don't know how long we'll have to stand being cooped up in here." She glanced around at the dim walls and shuddered. "They might have given us something cheery to live in," she added in disgust.

"Then you don't think we've been kidnapped for money?" Paula wanted to know.

Monica shook her head. "They wouldn't get very much money for us," she laughed shakily. "None of us is Mr. Denton's daughter, and even he isn't any millionaire."

"Audrey is right," Esther agreed. "They think we heard their plans and are making sure we don't broadcast them."

"I wonder if they have Jo-Jo here?" Monica asked suddenly, a wistful tone creeping into her voice that the girls couldn't help hearing.

"I doubt it," Audrey thought. "Although they seem to have had a place prepared for somebody," she added, looking round the cobwebby room again.

"They planned to stay up here themselves, I think," Monica replied. "Then decided it was as good a place as any for disposing of us."

"Maybe they will just ride off in the morning and leave us locked up here," Paula commented.

"You're a cheery soul, aren't you?" Esther chuckled, and then her smile faded as the grinding noise of the bolt being drawn back in the door told them all that someone was coming in.

It was Pedro who shuffled in holding a board on which were four small bowls of soup and some dry bread. He laid his home-made tray down and gazed at them through half-shut eyes, which his long, dank hair partially covered and then, still without speaking, turned and left the room bolting the door behind him.

The girls stared after him puzzled for they had been expecting harsh warnings and threats. Audrey felt more uneasy than ever for, somehow, that long silent look had seemed more menacing than any threats he had ever used.

"I don't get it," Audrey muttered, as they hungrily gathered round the bowls of soup. It wasn't very good soup but to the half-frozen girls, it tasted wonderful. "Maybe they are going to ride off in the morning and leave us, after all."

Monica yawned and shook her head to keep herself awake, after she had finished her soup. "Right now I wouldn't care if they ran off and left us tonight. I'm too sleepy to be frightened any more." The others nodded agreement and, before Audrey could think of another thing to talk about, Monica had rolled in wearily.

Audrey bowed her head and silently prayed. Somehow, she felt timid about saying anything aloud, but, when she raised her head she found Paula and Esther had been doing the same. They glanced at the already sleeping Monica and smiled to each other. She would understand soon if they had anything to do with it. But right now was not the time.

But even though they were bodily and mentally tired, the high wind and rain that battered the small window high in the wall, kept the other three awake for a long time afterwards. Audrey was the last to close her eyes after she had satisfied herself that everything was quiet downstairs, too.

The morning sun struck them harshly in the face the next morning and, struggling up, they found to their astonishment that it was nearly ten o'clock. All was quiet downstairs. Where were the men? Audrey would have given anything to know the answer to that question. Would Mr. Denton get the Sheriff on their trail right away—or would he know where to send him? She turned to Monica, who was returning from listening at the door for voices.

"How far away do you think we are?"

"I honestly don't know, Audrey," Monica replied wearily. "I knew where I was for quite a while and then they started to zig-zag back and forth, after we left the forest, and I really got mixed up." She shrugged. "We might actually be nearer home and then again . . ." she didn't finish but the girls got the general idea.

"I wonder where Jo-Jo is?" Paula said suddenly. "We're sure now that they've got him, but where could they have hidden him? Or was he one of the horses with us last night?"

"I couldn't say . . . it was so dark," Audrey replied.

"Jo-Jo wasn't there last night, I'm sure," Monica reassured them. "I would know him anywhere."

"All the horses were black . . . so that let's Jo-Jo out," Esther put in.

"If we only knew their plans," Audrey said worriedly.

"If we could only get a message through to Dad,"

Monica put in. "But I didn't have a thing on me that I could have dropped to leave a trail."

"I never even thought of it," Audrey confessed. "I was feeling too miserable."

"Well, the storm last night would have removed it anyway," Monica consoled her.

A shaft of light from the bright sun came down mockingly through the bars of the window and played on the girls' tired faces. Audrey looked up at it and felt frustrated. The mountain air was cool and fresh and just called to them to come outside and enjoy it. Monica saw her look up and followed her gaze.

"Maddening, isn't it?" she asked wryly, and then without any warning burst into tears. The sudden outburst was so unexpected that the three Canadians stared at their new friend in consternation.

Audrey put her arm around her and tried to comfort her. "Don't give up, Monica . . . we'll get out."

Monica blinked the tears from her eyes and smiled at them. "I'm not worrying so much about us, for we can try to get free . . . but it's Jo-Jo . . ." her voice broke on the name and the sobs started again. Paula and Esther glanced sympathetically at one another, while Audrey tried to smooth her rumpled hair back from her hot forehead. Audrey was at a loss for words. What could you say?

"We've been praying for you and Jo-Jo," she said earnestly, and Monica jerked her head up and looked at her through tear-filled eyes. "Haven't we?" she asked of Paula and Esther who nodded in unison. "Try to have faith in Him, Monica," she added fearfully. She was afraid of being snubbed again. But Monica just nodded.

"Yes, I know you have, Audrey. That's why I wasn't

so surprised when I won the silver cup." The girls exchanged glances. They thought Monica had forgotten what Audrey had told her in the hotel room, but apparently she hadn't.

"I'm sorry, but I feel I can't go and pray about these things like you folks," she said after a long pause while she tried to stifle her sobs. Her voice was still coming in strangled gasps. "I've never prayed for anything special . . . just the Lord's Prayer, you know."

"Well, He likes us to come to Him and tell Him our little worries and troubles," Audrey explained. "Just like your own dad likes you to come to him when you need help."

Monica stared at the floor while trying to recover from her bout of weeping. "I would like to, Audrey . . . really I would," she said. The girls knew she meant it, too. "But I can't go now, when I haven't bothered about Him before, can I?"

"Yes, you can," Paula broke in eagerly. "He is always waiting for you to come to Him. Remember what Mr. Randall said," she added.

"Yes. Mr. Randall was right. One thing we can be very sure of is that Our Heavenly Father never forsakes anyone," Audrey hurriedly added. "All you have to do is pray to Him at any time and He will always answer you."

"That's right," Esther agreed. "Ye shall seek Me and find Me, when ye shall search for Me with all your heart," she quoted.

"I've always believed," Monica went on thoughtfully. "But I never thought of asking Him to help me in any special kind of way before . . . it sounds wonderful," she added wistfully.

"In God have I put my trust: I will not be afraid

what man can do unto me," Audrey quoted also. "**And believe me, this is one situation that can prove whether you really want to believe or not,**" she added meaningfully.

Monica smiled and opened her mouth to ask a question when the voices of the men downstairs interrupted the conversation. The girls stiffened into silence and waited while their hearts pounded excitedly. There were footsteps now on the stairs, then the grating sound of the bolt and, again, Pedro entered with a laden tray of food which he carefully laid on the rickety table.

As he turned to leave again, he glared at them all in turn. "Tonight, we move on," he snarled in a guttural tone of voice and Audrey shuddered at the cruelness of the man's face.

"Where are we going?" Monica asked defiantly.

Pedro turned slowly round and looked at her. The girls swallowed nervously as a malicious smile slid over the heavy-lined face.

"Never you mind," he growled. "You weel know soon." He turned and silently left the room without a backward glance, leaving the four girls looking at his retreating back and then at each other in dismay.

"Monica! We've got to get out of here before tonight," Audrey whispered fiercely. "They must be going to take us over the Border with them, just as you said they would."

"I don't know which would be worse . . . having to go with them or staying here alone in this tower," Paula groaned.

Monica nodded and looked at Audrey. "How can we get out, Audrey? Just look at the size of that window."

The four looked up at it again and felt the hope-lessness of it all overtake them. With a sigh Audrey turned away and went over to the table.

"Let's eat first," she suggested. "We might get inspired if we have some food in us."

The girls sat down and reluctantly ate the rather doughy biscuits and scorched fried eggs that the tray contained, while Audrey frowned thoughtfully up at the window.

"Even if we did get out, we would be seen right away," she observed darkly.

"Maybe we can make a break for it when they take us out of here," Monica out in.

"If even one of us could just get away . . . we could bring help," Paula said eagerly.

There was a long pause and then Esther spoke. "Isn't there some way we could get those bars removed?" The others looked at her in silence. "If we only had a file," she added wearily.

"Even if we had a file how could we use it?" Monica asked. "The sawing sound would be heard for miles in this warm air."

"Well, we haven't a file . . . so that takes care of that," Audrey laughed ruefully. She glanced up again at the window and then getting up, she removed every-thing from the table and pulled it under the window, placing the one and only battered chair on top of that. Climbing up she peeked out. The air was sweet and cool and gave her fresh courage and hope.

"I never knew how lovely everything was outdoors until I got locked inside a room," she called down to them. "Everything is so peaceful."

"It won't be for long," Monica moaned. "I can't see those men making life peaceful for anyone."

"I wonder what the folks are doing about finding us?" Paula asked. "We've been gone all night, so they know something has happened to us."

"In a state as vast as this, it isn't very easy to guess where someone has disappeared to," Monica told her. "Probably Dad and Mr. Denton are racking their brains trying to figure out where we went to."

"Well, they'll never think of an old disused monastery, I'm sure," Esther groaned.

"They might think of the Mexican Border," Audrey called down.

"The border being about three or four thousand miles long will give them some problem," Monica gloomed. "I'm not trying to be pessimistic," she added.

"Well, you're not doing bad at that," Audrey laughed wryly. Somehow the sight of outdoors, even through a window, was giving her courage.

The rolling countryside was void of any human being on it as far as she could see. What she had said before had been true. Even if they could escape, they would be easily noticed running across that lonely stretch of ground. The trees that had shaded them a little the night before were a long distance off, and by the time they tried to get under their protection the men would have easily caught up with them. A stamping sound suddenly caught her ears and, glancing sideways, she saw that four horses were tied near the door that they had entered in. She looked down at her chums.

"There are four horses at the door but I don't see any of the men," she whispered.

"Is Jo-Jo there?" Monica asked wistfully and sighed when Audrey shook her head.

"They're all blacks. Have a look for yourself," she invited, stepping off the chair on to the table and pulling Monica up beside her. The other two girls climbed on to the table beside Audrey. They could just see the horses and no more.

Esther giggled nervously as she clung to Paula. "It's a good thing this old table is made of solid oak or . . ." she broke off when Monica gasped.

"One of the horses down there is Jo-Jo," she whispered half to herself. "Some horse faker must have coloured him, but I'd know the toss of that head anywhere."

The others peered over the edge of the sill and saw the black horses stamping impatiently, but they all looked the same. Suddenly Monica pursed her lips and whistled gently. The girls held their breaths and watched and gasped in delight when one of the horses pricked up his ears and stamped gently on the ground with his front hoof. It was Jo-Jo!

Again Monica whistled and this time Jo-Jo, although black and with his tail tied up like the others, pranced excitedly, whinnying gently.

"The men will hear you," Esther gasped nervously.

"No they won't. There they are over there!" Monica whispered back and pointed. The three girls could just make out the figures of the three men in the far distance climbing up on the rocks at the side of the long stretch of land.

Again Monica whistled and this time called quietly. "Come, Jo-Jo! Come!" The voice, though low, was commanding and the horse sensed the urgency in it. Pressing back on his rope, he tugged gently—then waited. Again Monica called. Jo-Jo whinnied then and suddenly threw his head back with a jerk causing the rope that held him to snap. Jo-Jo was free!

"Now he can go home," Monica breathed thankfully.

"Give Jo-Jo your scarf, Monica. Quick!" Audrey's frantic voice penetrated the girl's senses and with a great hope, she tore off a large red, white and blue silk scarf that she had worn at the Rodeo and pushed it through the bars, letting it float gently earthward.

Jo-Jo came over and stood still. Monica called gently. "Pick it up, Jo-Jo!" Jo-Jo hesitated, flicking his ears. "Jo-Jo! Pick it up!" Monica's voice was commanding again. The horse tossed his head, walked over to the scarf and picked it up and stood waiting. Audrey felt weak from nervousness. She whispered into Monica's ear.

Monica nodded. "Jo-Jo! Go home! Quick! Home! Jo-Jo, go home!"

At the last command Jo-Jo turned and with a toss of his lovely head, started off briskly, then as if feeling his way, slowed up again. The girls watched in agonised impatience. Would the men come back and see him? Then Jo-Jo, as if quite sure now, tossed his head once more and broke into a gallop, disappearing from sight in a few minutes.

A Prayer Answered

11 AFTER JO-JO HAD GONE, THE GIRLS slipped quickly from the table again to the floor in case the men would return and catch them watching. They were still shaking from nervous excitement. Would Jo-Jo be spotted in the distance? These men had been on the rocks and might see him, although Audrey noticed they had disappeared before Jo-Jo had left.

Suddenly a thought struck her. "Monica! What were the men doing on those rocks over there?" she asked.

Monica took a deep breath. The sight of her pet had knocked the breath out of her. She swallowed. "They are probably watching the Patrols at the Border through field glasses. We can only be a stone's throw away from it. Getting everything lined up for tonight, no doubt."

"I wonder if they saw Jo-Jo?" Paula shivered excitedly.

"If they did, they'll still have to hurry back here and get their mounts before they can chase after him . . . and I'm quite sure they can't catch him," Monica replied, her face almost happy-looking now, although the grim expression hadn't completely disappeared yet. There was still the danger they were in themselves when the men came back and found the horse was gone.

"They won't blame us, will they?" Esther asked. "When they find Jo-Jo gone, I mean."

"No. How can they? But we'll probably pay for it

with their temper and rage," Audrey returned worriedly. "Oh, I hope Jo-Jo makes it home. Your Dad will know what has happened, won't he?"

Monica nodded. "Sure. I only hope he orders Jo-Jo to find me. We've trained him to hunt for me . . . and he always has found me."

"We're so far away from home though, aren't we?" Paula asked. "Maybe he won't find his way back so easily."

"Now who's not having faith," Monica put in, and Paula laughed.

The hours went by but still the men did not return to the monastery. The girls were getting more uneasy every minute. What had happened to them? Had they already been caught?

"Shouldn't Jo-Jo have been back with help by now?" Esther asked. "It has been quite a while since he left."

Monica shook her head. "It's a little soon yet, Esther. Look how long it took us to get here, and Jo-Jo has all the way back to come."

"It will be awful if our dads don't understand that Jo-Jo left us and didn't just break loose himself," Paula put in.

"I'm sure Jo-Jo will make them understand. After all, the scarf should give them a clue," Monica explained.

"Oh, I forgot all about the scarf," Paula replied relieved. "Maybe the men have decided not to come back and have left us to starve to death," she added.

"They wouldn't leave their horses," Monica replied firmly. "They wouldn't find such good ones again. Besides, they wouldn't want anything to happen to us on this side of the Border."

"What could have happened to them?" Audrey groaned. "I don't like the looks of it."

"Frankly, neither do I," Monica agreed seriously and added morosely. "It's getting so dark and I'm getting hungry."

Suddenly Audrey's head bowed and her voice spoke quietly and clearly in the tower room.

"Dear Heavenly Father. You know the danger we are in. Please, help us! Show us what we can do to help ourselves. Take care of us, please. We ask it in Jesus' Name . . . Amen."

When she raised her head she saw Monica raise hers, too, and gaze across at her with a startled but thoughtful look on her face. Esther and Paula smiled over to Audrey, understanding written on their faces.

"This is a test for us, too, I guess," Paula declared solemnly and Esther agreed.

Still the time went by and the rays of the sun disappeared from the little window, leaving only a glow. The lengthening shadows in the room only added to the depressed state of the girls' minds.

"I wonder if Jo-Jo found his way back home all right?" Paula asked, breaking the silence that seemed to have become permanent.

"He'll go back the way that the Mexicans brought him," Monica replied. "All I hope is that our folks get here in time."

Audrey looked at her sharply in the semi-dark room. "Do you think they'll be back soon . . . the Mexicans, I mean?"

"I think that they'll wait till the very last minute before coming to get us," Monica replied.

"What difference would that make?" Esther wanted to know.

"So that we won't have time to ask too many questions," Monica told her.

Hunger was beginning to make the girls jumpy. The awful waiting was telling even on their cast-iron nerves. If they only knew what was before them, Audrey reflected grimly, then they could make some kind of plan.

"Maybe your Dad won't recognise your scarf, Monica," Esther put in suddenly.

"He might not, but Mrs. Denton will," Monica replied. "She gave it to me for Christmas last year."

The conversation lagged again. It seemed so hard to keep up a cheerful optimistic air when you kept wondering all the time when it would soon be over. Monica and Audrey were sitting on the edge of the bed gazing up at the window wearily, and Esther sat on the broken-down chair while Paula leaned against the table with her arms folded.

"I know one thing," Monica said grimly. "When they are taking us away, really put up a fight for it this time. We were taken by surprise the last time."

"Don't worry . . . we're prepared this time," Audrey returned, equally as grim.

It was just then that a strange sound hit their ears. They looked at each other and then up to the window where the sound had come from. It was faraway but clear. But what on earth was it?

Jumping up from the bed, Audrey, with Paula's help, drew the table over again under the window. Quickly ascending, she peered out between the bars. At first, she couldn't see anything at all. Darkness was now falling rapidly and only light shadows touched the hills in the distance making the long stretches of ground seem patchy in between, but nothing moved.

"What is it?" Monica asked sharply, as she gazed up at her.

Audrey shook her head. "I don't know. I can't see a thing. It sounds like voices or music, doesn't it?"

"Maybe it's our own folks with help," Esther declared happily, but her face sobered when Audrey again shook her head.

"I don't think it's coming from the same direction that Jo-Jo went," she replied.

"I'll have a look with you," Monica declared, climbing up beside her while Paula and Esther followed suit, holding the chair for Monica to stand on for a better view.

Then the sound came again from the distance. It was a cross between a whine and a roar. It was drawing nearer and nearer but still nothing was visible. The girls stood clinging to each other and watching cautiously, their eyes roving over the lonely scene outside. The horses below had now heard it and were whinnying nervously and pawing the ground. The sight unnerved the girls even more. It was actually frightening the horses whatever it was. What on earth could it be and why didn't it appear?

Suddenly Monica grabbed Audrey's arm. "It's Pedro and his men!" she gasped in horror and nearly fell off the chair in her excitement. "They must be drunk or something," she explained, for the others couldn't see quite so far from where they stood on the table. "Just listen!"

Audrey closed her eyes for a moment. What terrible thing would they do when they found that Jo-Jo was gone? How would they vent their rage? The men were now in sight of them all. They were shouting and singing and trying to run. Gusts of their coarse laughter floated menacingly up to the four girls shuddering in terror.

Closer and closer they came toward the monastery, looking wildly savage in that peculiar twilight. Now they were at the door. Would they notice Jo-Jo was gone? The girls held their breaths while Monica pressed her face closer to the bars to see what they would do. But they didn't once glance in the direction of the horses, but plunged through the heavy door laughing at something. They hadn't noticed!

Their coarse voices were now shouting to each other in Spanish and Monica had no trouble in hearing what they said. Her already pale face was white as she bent close to the other three and whispered.

"They're going to take us over the Border at midnight and lose us somewhere in Mexico . . . just what I thought they would do."

"Well, that's good. Now all we have to do is find our way home after they leave us," Audrey replied happily but Monica shook her head.

"You don't know Mexico, Audrey. We'll never get back to the States. Don't forget they'll take us to the very roughest part of the city they choose . . . and then we won't get any help. We'll be the foreigners then."

The men's shouting conversation had now turned into an argument and sounded twice as bad as before. The girls didn't know what it was all about and even Monica stood uncertain.

"One of them is afraid to go on with it, I think," she whispered. "The others are threatening him."

The voices rose up and down in anger, and the girls cowered behind the big door and tried not to look afraid, so as to give the others courage.

Suddenly there was quietness and the girls looked

at one another in wonder. What had happened now? It was Monica who guessed.

"They've gone out to the horses now and . . ." she broke off and swallowed. Audrey steeled herself for what was coming. The men would know now that Jo-Jo had gone and be really angry.

It was then that Audrey got a bright idea. Silently gesturing to the others to help her, she pointed to the table and then to the door. The girls silently nodded and together they pushed and shoved the heavy lumbering piece of wood over and set it under the handle of the door.

The bed was next to be moved and proved almost too much for them. But desperation made them work harder. Soon, it too, joined the table. Even the chair was placed on top of the pile. The four, panting breathlessly, tried to straighten their backs from the heavy task of pushing and pulling, when the men's voices sounded once more. They stood rigidly waiting.

Audrey couldn't hear anything distinctly now for the pounding of her heart, but she did know that the men were now clambering and falling up the stairs toward their door. As they stumbled to the top, the door was unbolted and the handle turned and then silence as the four girls pushed silently on the piled furniture. The men outside seemed puzzled at first and then it dawned on them what had happened.

Audrey closed her eyes as the men began pounding and shouting angrily through the door at them. Their voices snarling in rage as the heavily-barred door withstood their heavy assault on it. Audrey didn't know what they were saying, but at the expression of Monica's face she could imagine.

"Hold everything tight, girls!" Audrey whispered

and all four put their weight beside the bed while the men pushed from outside. Several times the door cracked open a trifle, but was hastily shut again by the girls. Audrey knew they couldn't keep this up long for already their strength was waning.

"Oh, dear Father . . . save us, please!" This fervent prayer was jerked from Monica's white lips as the door again peeped open with the pressure from the men.

Again and again they tried, with the men getting the door open a little more with each new siege on it. It was just when the girls felt that they could no longer take it, that a thundering sound from outside was heard quite plainly. The men stopped pushing for a moment as if they were listening, too. It sounded like hoofbeats. Could it be . . .? It was! It was horses! They were distinct now and they were coming nearer. A cry of thankfulness broke from Audrey as the men began to fall and scramble back down the stairs.

A shout from below, a scuffle, and then silence. Now voices were heard as someone came back up the stairs. Audrey felt her throat go dry with horror. They were coming back!

It was Esther's voice that snapped her attention. "It's Dad!" Her loud shout brought an answering one from outside. Mr. Chapman's voice! Weak from relief, they frantically tore away their barricade and opened the door. There stood Mr. Chapman, Mr. Denton and Mr. Dean with smiles on their white, worried faces.

"Where's Dad?" Monica asked anxiously, peering round her in the hall.

"Downstairs with Jo-Jo, Monica," Mr. Denton laughed somewhat shakily. "I thought Jo-Jo was coming up the stairs with us. He couldn't get us back here quick enough. We hardly knew him in his new colour, but that will soon be taken care of."

The four girls hurried down the stairs and outside with the men behind them. There stood Jo-Jo with Mr. Evans's hand on his head. Monica skimmed the distance between them, flinging herself onto Jo-Jo and hugging him. Jo-Jo rolled his eyes and backed down in one of his very best bows. It brought a laugh to everyone.

Mr. Evans's usual smiling face was strained, but Monica grabbed his arm in relief swinging him around.

"You'll never know just how nearly too late you were, Dad," she explained ungrammatically. "One more push against that door and we just couldn't have made it."

"Where's the . . .?" Audrey's question was answered by her dad who pointed in the distance to five horsemen.

"The Sheriff and his aide were real happy to come along with us when we phoned and told him that Jo-Jo had returned with Monica's scarf between his teeth."

"Dad! Did you tell Jo-Jo to come and find me?" Monica asked, as they all rode slowly back to Little Creek Ranch.

Mr. Evans laughed. "Didn't need to, my dear. Jo-Jo just tossed his head and kept pawing the ground for us to follow him."

"I hope his new owner takes good care of him," Monica said so wistfully that it touched the hearts of her three friends beside her.

"I heard that, Monica!" Mr. Denton shouted back from where he was leading the group homewards. "Jo-Jo is not going anywhere. I wouldn't be the one to split up a partnership like that for any amount of money."

Monica's face simply glowed with happiness at this news. She turned to Audrey and nodded.

"Your prayers have been answered." She silently rode for a moment and then spoke quietly so that only her three new friends could hear her. "And in more ways than one. I'm going to be a real Christian, too, from now on, believe me. Now I see the difference between really knowing Him and just being merely aware of Him. Tonight I'll take the Lord Jesus Christ as my own."

The three Canadians rode on with contented hearts. Monica understood now! Suddenly Esther, who was riding in the rear with Paula, whispered.

"Isn't it great! Now we have another witness for Christ!

Paula nodded. "Yes. And we have made the acquaintance of a wonderful horse, named Jo-Jo, who helped us."